Lifting the Veil
Temptation Unveiled

R.G. ALEXANDER

ELLORA'S CAVE
ROMANTICA PUBLISHING

An Ellora's Cave Romantica Publication

www.ellorascave.com

Lifting the Veil

ISBN 9781419963513
ALL RIGHTS RESERVED.
Lifting the Veil Copyright © 2008 R.G. Alexander
Edited by Briana St. James.
Cover art by Syneca.

Electronic book publication April 2008
Trade paperback publication 2011

With the exception of quotes used in reviews, this book may not be reproduced or used in whole or in part by any means existing without written permission from the publisher, Ellora's Cave Publishing, Inc.® 1056 Home Avenue, Akron OH 44310-3502.

Warning: The unauthorized reproduction or distribution of this copyrighted work is illegal. Criminal copyright infringement, including infringement without monetary gain, is investigated by the FBI and is punishable by up to 5 years in federal prison and a fine of $250,000.
(http://www.fbi.gov/ipr/)

This book is a work of fiction and any resemblance to persons, living or dead, or places, events or locales is purely coincidental. The characters are productions of the author's imagination and used fictitiously.

LIFTING THE VEIL
ಚಿ

Dedication

To Cookie – love is the reason.

Acknowledgements

Thank you to my husband and sister for their unconditional love and support. Eden Bradley, Crystal Jordan and Lillian Feisty for hand-holding above and beyond the call of duty. Robin L. Rotham – advisor extraordinaire. And to The Romance Divas – for everything – thank you.

Trademarks Acknowledgement

The author acknowledges the trademarked status and trademark owners of the following wordmarks mentioned in this work of fiction:

Super Bowl: NFL
Wolverine: Marvel Comics

When my time has long gone
And the gods that once sheltered and
Governed the earth have turned away
When the human race has forgotten Magick,
Forgotten themselves
Complacent in their ignorance...
That is when the danger will strike.

Translation from the Ogham Book of Veils, as prophesied by Áine, High Priestess of Danu.

Chapter One
ೞ

"A singing strip-o-gram?"

Meru Tanner dogged her aunt's steps as the tall, slender woman searched behind the counter for her purse.

"A choir of drunken off-duty police officers serenading me with raunchy ditties at two o'clock in the morning? What, Aunt Lily? What morally corrupt and thoroughly humiliating plan has Sheridan cooked up to celebrate my official descent into spinsterhood?"

"Aha!" Lily pulled the elusive handbag from under a pile of order forms and Meru huffed her exasperation. "Sorry, dear, your cousin swore me to secrecy. Besides, thirty is not the end of the road, thank you very much." She tried to look down her nose indignantly, spoiling it with a mischievous wink. "I think I'd better leave before you torture it out of me. Anyway, all this talk about your birthday reminded me how much I have to do before tonight."

"Tonight?" Meru tilted her head.

"Yes, silly goose. Tonight at midnight, just like every August first at midnight, we form the circle in the yard behind the shop. To celebrate Lugh's Wedding."

Meru's eyes rounded in barely concealed horror. She had forgotten.

She hadn't been around on the anniversary of her birth in years, hadn't lived in the tiny one-room apartment above the store since they'd first moved to Houston and were getting her aunt's metaphysical shop, The Willow's Knot, off the ground.

Now, however, she was renting the space while she decided what she was going to do with her life since she'd left graduate school, and her career in academia, behind. She should have remembered.

Four times a year, Aunt Lily faithfully formed a Druid circle, honoring her ancestors and communing with nature. There was Samhain, Imbolg, Bealtaine and Lughnassadh, or Lugh's wedding. They were celebrated on and around the dates of each solstice and equinox.

Meru's birthday just happened to fall on one of them. According to her birth certificate, she was born at midnight on August first. At the last stroke of midnight, if Lily was to be believed, a fact she loved telling her fellow pagans. From the awed and interested expressions on their faces when they looked at her, she wasn't sure if she was supposed to sprout horns or turn water into wine.

"Should I go hang out at the house?"

Thankfully, Lily was oblivious to the hopeful note in her voice. "Well, we're all meeting there after the ritual. But you're more than welcome to join us, love. Everyone is always asking about you."

Meru's shoulders hunched in defeat, though she had to smile. Eleven excitable New Age Druids and one audacious hostess—a mosh pit might be a bit more relaxing. At least the shop was closed tomorrow.

"All right, I'm off." Her aunt put on the shoes she only wore when forced by the hot Houston asphalt. "My friend Izzy said my aura has been full of purple lately, so she offered to dye a few streaks to match before the ceremony."

She held up several strands of her light brown hair and Meru laughed. "Have fun."

"I always do, my dearest." Lily blew her a kiss and then disappeared in the cloud of sandalwood and happy chaos that always surrounded her.

A few hours later, after serving several dozen customers, Meru walked the perimeter of the store, straightening and dusting as she went.

She still blushed to think about the odd little man who'd bought out their entire stock of Horned God Elixir. Of all the things she'd ever imagined herself doing, hawking an herbal remedy for erectile dysfunction that advertised itself as "the perfect way to RISE to the occasion" was definitely not among them.

Aunt Lily really had something special in The Willow's Knot. In keeping with a Celtic theme, the store was imbued with rich tones of purple, gold and green. The trim was alive with swirling and complex Celtic knots. The chairs and shelving were made from a warm, knobby wood. It had always felt so magical in here. If the popularity of the shop was anything to go by, the customers felt it as well. It was home.

Her aunt had added new merchandise in the last couple of years. There were rows of crystal chakra bowls near the old mortar and pestle. Shelves were lined with healing herbs, bronze censers and small colored candles for spell-work. On the opposite wall, books, music and subliminal self help tapes climbed up from the floor, seeming cozy instead of cluttered.

The large, circular display area in the middle was her favorite…the divination section. The lower part of the display was crammed with packaged fortunes. Tarot cards of every ilk, I Ching kits, runes and pendulums filled each available nook.

The tabletop was one of Lily's strokes of genius. People were immediately drawn to the open bag of Ogham runes and the Faerie cards spread out in an enticing fan. Anyone who passed could draw a rune or card at random and look at the tiny definition booklets that lay beside them.

As a teenager, whenever she was worried about a test, hung up on a boy or simply out of sorts, she would always find her way to this display. Trying out whatever set of cards or runes her aunt had out at the time, searching for answers. Though she knew logically that most fortune-telling paraphernalia was more a clarifying tool than a clairvoyant one, it had always helped.

Here I am again, she chuckled. A few hours from thirty, still unsure of herself and where she was going, still wondering if she would ever have something or someone special of her own.

Her family was right. She should stop being so nitpicky about the men she dated. She should take Sher up on her offer and go out with Bob, the fireman she'd been trying to set her up with.

They didn't understand. Didn't know how badly she had chosen not too long ago. She couldn't make that mistake again. Oh, they'd known she was dating Allen for a month or two while pursuing her doctorate, but thankfully, they hadn't questioned her when she'd told them they'd parted ways and decided to remain friends. Thank God. She was just too ashamed to tell them the truth.

She knew real love existed. Even though they'd died in a car accident when she was three years old, she remembered that her parents had been madly in love.

Aunt Lily had been in love as well. But three weeks before Sheridan's birth nearly thirty-one years ago, Lily's young husband had passed away. She had yet to be in another long-term relationship. And it wasn't from lack of suitors. Everyone loved Lily.

But whenever Meru asked her about it, Lily would just smile in a dreamy far off way. "You will realize soon enough, Meru, that the women of our family only fall in love once. And that fall lasts forever."

Then she'd shake herself sloughing off the morbid thought and winking naughtily as she added, "Lust, however, can strike anywhere and at anytime."

Meru placed her hand in the large hemp pouch and felt the cool, smooth wood against her fingers.

These weren't ordinary Nordic style runes like the small stone-shaped pewter pieces she was used to. Aunt Lily had actually purchased these from an artisan she met at The

Renaissance Faire a few years ago. A giant of a man with the hands of Michelangelo, she'd claimed. Shaped like staves, or sticks, the carefully polished strips of ash were engraved with Ogham script.

Ogham was thought to be the ancient written language of the Celts. Perhaps even of the Druids themselves. Meru had learned to decipher it at a very young age, to impress her aunt mostly, but also because she had been fascinated by the markings.

Closing her eyes in concentration, she pulled one from the bag. Even knowing what the symbol meant, she still dutifully leafed through the booklet until she found the divinatory meaning.

"New Beginnings." Her voice rose over the Andean flute music that played soft in the background. "Purification and Initiation. The start of a new adventure or project. Clean away the old and be open to all new possibilities."

It certainly did feel like she was starting over. Although the last few months she'd been in a sort of holding pattern, as if she was waiting for...something.

The bell over the door chimed its merry tune. She glanced up quickly, a smile of genuine delight shaping her lips as she recognized the newcomers.

"Professor White! What a wonderful surprise! And Fletcher too, of course, how are you?"

The two older men nodded in greeting as they made their way over. Professor White had become a familiar and beloved face. He was always stopping by to purchase some little knickknack and he could rarely resist pulling up a stool and staying for hours to flirt with Lily or share a lively debate with Meru. They discovered shortly after they'd met that they shared one all-consuming obsession — mythology.

He seemed to be an expert on just about every culture's mythos, giving Meru many sleepless nights of research just to keep up with him. She loved it. It was what she missed most about life at the university—the heated debates and shared excitement of discovery, the sheer fascination with knowledge that, thankfully, the old man shared.

Fletcher was some sort of nurse or companion to the aged professor. He hovered like a mother hen over his charge, always no more than a raised voice away as far as Meru had seen.

She and Fletcher had always had a rather tense relationship, though she'd never understood why. She constantly tried to put him at ease, but though Fletcher was never exactly rude to her, he seemed to hold himself back from relaxing around her. To be fair, he seemed uncomfortable around everyone but the professor.

Professor White took Meru's hand and gallantly pressed it to his lips, his unique silver eyes twinkling up at her impishly. "Meru, you look lovely as always. Where is everyone? Has that delightful goddess abandoned you this afternoon?"

She chuckled and wagged her finger at the older man. "Your secret is out now, Professor. You don't come here to see me at all, do you? You're really after Aunt Lily, just like every other Romeo who walks through that door. Well, you're out of luck today, I'm afraid. She's off dyeing purple streaks in her hair before tonight's gathering."

"Purple, hmm?" the professor's rich voice lowered. "How...intriguing."

Meru and Fletcher rolled their eyes simultaneously at the slightly glazed expression on his wrinkled face. She led the way back toward the counter, where several stools had been set to the side for her favorite visitors.

"So, what brings you by today, Professor? I haven't gotten any new orders with your name on them. Are you expecting anything?" She watched as he hopped on the stool with surprising agility.

He caught her eye and raised one bushy eyebrow in surprise. "Are you sure, Ms. Tanner? Will you check once more, to put my old mind at ease?"

She nodded and ducked down to the cabinet below where most of the customer's orders were usually stored. Sure enough, sitting right on top of the pile, was a rather hefty square package for Prof. M. White.

"I could've sworn..." she mumbled to herself before lifting it onto the glass counter "I'm so sorry for—"

The professor waved her efforts away with a kind smile.

"Dear girl, it is I who must apologize to you." He assured her. "I sent away for this item ages ago. Only just remembered it was coming today. I know I'm getting far too old to bear when I almost forget the birthday of a beautiful young woman like you."

She looked up quickly. "How did you know it was my birthday?" As far as she knew, the topic had never come up.

"I have my ways, dear Meru." He chuckled at some private joke until Fletcher harrumphed quietly beside him, nudging him with a not-so-subtle prod of his elbow.

"Sorry, dear," he grinned unabashedly. "Leave me my little secrets and enjoy the gift in the spirit in which it was given."

When she reached for the brown wrapping concealing her prize, a gnarled, yet surprisingly strong hand, covered her own.

"Unless I am mistaken, your birthday doesn't officially begin until midnight." She blushed and drew her hand away. What in the world had the professor gotten her? Her vision blurred and she felt a lump form in her throat. Other than her aunt and Sher, when was the last time anyone had gotten her anything?

"What a wonderful surprise, Professor!" She came around the counter and gave him a quick but heartfelt hug. "I don't know how to thank you." She pulled away in time to see a rosy color suffuse the skin above his beard. He gave her an awkward pat, as if unused to physical affection.

"That is more than thanks enough, my girl." He responded gruffly before standing in preparation to leave. "Fletcher and I have a lot to do this evening. Not the hullabaloo Lily has planned, I'm sure, but we'll bake some bread and invite our friend Raj over to join us."

She smiled and nodded. "How is Raj? I haven't seen him in weeks."

Since getting to know the professor, she'd had come to his large Victorian several times for dinner and conversation. Very often they were joined by Raj, quite possibly the most beautiful man she had ever seen.

He was also one of the most intelligent, and Meru often wondered why she couldn't fall for someone like him. But even if he looked at her with as much interest as he did the old worn books that always surrounded him, she'd never felt anything beyond friendship for the quiet, introspective man.

"He's fine, just fine. Doing some research for a little project of mine."

Her interest perked — a little research would certainly take her mind off her lack of social life. "Anything I can help with, Professor?"

The old man chuckled again as he turned and walked slowly toward the door.

"Could be, Ms. Tanner, could be. Time will tell." At the door, he paused, Fletcher patiently holding it open for him as he met her smiling gaze. "I trust you'll be able to control your curiosity, at least until midnight."

He glanced at the package and then smiled at her look of consternation. "Oh, and try to have fun tomorrow. It is, after all, a very special day." He walked away with a wave and Meru thought she heard him say, "A day of possibilities."

* * * * *

"So, are they naked?"

"What? No, Sheridan, they aren't...okay, George and Helen are, but everyone else is decent." Meru cradled the phone between her shoulder and ear, walking toward the microwave as it beeped. She took out the steaming bag of popcorn with one hand, holding it carefully by the edge as she grabbed a soda from the fridge with the other.

"I'm not telling you anything else." She paused to blow a dark brown curl away from her face in aggravation before plopping back into her front-row seat by the window and popping open the can for a sip. "This isn't the Super Bowl. It's a very serious, spiritual event."

"So is the Super Bowl, depending on who you ask," Sheridan quipped.

"Besides, I'm stuck in this stinky bachelor-mobile of Kyle's on yet another boring stakeout. The most exciting thing our perp has done all day is clean out his cat box." Sheridan's partner responded rudely in the background and her cousin laughed.

"I'm so sorry you're bored, Sher. Those inconsiderate criminals! Don't they know you have better things to do than wait on them...like driving your cousin crazy with ridiculous questions?"

They both chuckled.

"Speaking of questions, I heard you were trying, and not very successfully, to pry info out of Mom about your birthday."

"I don't know what you're talking about."

"Whatever, Cuz. Just be ready when I pick you up tomorrow night. Wear the blue dress Mom bought for you last year."

Meru snorted, and then winced as soda bubbles shot up her nose. Setting the can down quickly, she leapt up to grab a paper towel from the counter. "No way, Sheridan the

Harridan," she said between sniffs. "I have washcloths that cover more of my skin."

Meru walked back to the window and her lips twitched in amusement. *Time to go for the distraction.*

Feigning a shocked gasp, she cried, "Oh my lord, will you look at that? They've tied a goat to a tree near the circle."

There was a moment's silence on the other end of the line. "Okay, this is when you tell me you're joking. Mom and her crew have always been crazy...but even *she* would never—"

"She said this year they'd planned something a little different but—oh no! Aunt Lily's walking toward it with a—is that a *butcher* knife?" Meru smirked and hung up slowly to Sheridan's screeching. *"What?* Wait, Meru—"

Sighing, she snuggled comfortably in the papasan chair near the window. Nibbling on her salty treat, she pondered her cousin's hostile reaction to all things supernatural. She hadn't always been that way. But ever since that Halloween all those years ago...well, since that day, Sheridan had no time for anything magical. And her mother had decided not to press the issue.

It was around that time that Lily had stopped teaching them the ways of the Druids or expecting them to participate in any of the seasonal rituals. It had become the only sore spot between the mother and daughter, especially after Sheridan became an angst-filled teen. Meru couldn't help but feel guilty for her part in that rift.

She looked down at the small enclosed yard below and smiled. The Druids seemed to be starting the circle a bit early tonight. George and Helen were in fact naked. The others were dressed in everything from dramatic white robes to jeans.

Aunt Lily looked comfortable in linen pants and a short-sleeved lavender shirt that matched the streaks in her hair to perfection. She raised her hands to quiet the circle.

"We call on Lugh. Lugh of the Long Arm, Lugh of the True Light. Guide us with your fire." Three of the men in the circle came forward and lit the wood in the firepit.

"We call on Danu, Mother of us all, Goddess of the Waters, the True Queen. Fill us with your wisdom." Three women carrying urns came forward and poured water into the waiting trench around the fire. "Guide and protect us this night of all nights. Guide and protect your gatekeepers!"

Meru shivered suddenly and felt a strange sort of electricity all around her, standing the fine hairs of her arm on end.

Putting down her popcorn and setting her drink on the ledge, she stood and walked away from the window. She could hear the people below her beginning a low chant, though she couldn't make out what they were saying.

Her gaze fell on the countertop where she'd set Professor White's package, then flew up to the clock on the stove. Just after eleven. On the East Coast it was already her birthday. She wondered if that counted.

With hands that seemed unable to help themselves, she tore open her gift and gasped in delight. A book. One of the most beautiful she'd ever seen.

Lifting the large volume in her hands, she heaved an amorous sigh at the cool, satiny feel of the leather binding, which was buttery smooth with age. Intricate knotwork designs had been burned into the cover, and there, in the middle, the distinctive lines of writing she had seen just this afternoon. Ogham.

Where on earth had the professor gotten this? Her trained eye told her this was no reproduction, regardless of its good condition. She laid it open under the harsh kitchen lighting and leafed carefully through the pages.

Moments later, her brow furrowed in confusion. The obviously delicate paper that, she would guess, was made from hazelwood—a powerful and mystical tree in Celtic mythology—was blank. Totally, completely blank. Was it some sort of ancient diary that had never been filled? And why was the cover written in Ogham?

She looked at the empty book in consternation. Seconds later, she lay on the floor of her small living room, a language reference book and her mysterious gift in front of her. It only took a few moments to verify her translation. She traced the title on the cover with her finger, breathing the words aloud. "The Book of Veils."

Her heart pounded as she turned the tome over and around, trying desperately to see if there were any other markings that would give her a bit more information. A small scrap of paper fluttered from between the book's pages, landing in her lap.

"Curiouser and curiouser."

She shook her head with a chuckle, though her pulse tripped as she studied the clue. The scrap appeared to have been torn out of a similarly aged book. It too looked authentic and quite fragile. And there was writing on it, also in Ogham. The script, thankfully, was legible.

She grabbed some notebook paper and set to work, wondering all the while just what the professor had given her. She was dying to run over to his house and demand to know right now where he'd procured such an invaluable find. Something like this should be in a museum.

Her excitement grew as she worked. "A spell. It's a spell."

An actual Druid spell. Wouldn't the gathering downstairs have a fit if they knew what she had in her hot little hands?

"Lifting the Veil...of...Worlds." She mumbled under her breath as her pen flew across the paper. It had to be the fastest translation she had ever done. When she looked up again, only forty-five minutes had passed and she had somehow correctly translated the short entry. She knew she was right to her very bones.

It was a Druid invocation that allowed the user to alter their ordinary perceptions in order to see what it called "Others", or those from other realms, as well as their "Magick".

Anticipation hummed through her body, leaving her breathless. Near panting as she paced, notebook in hand, she laughed at herself. Giddy as a kid in a candy store, just because this so-called spell appeared to be the answer to nearly every childhood dream she'd ever had — to be in the know, to see the magic, to be special.

She'd read countless similar Native American and pagan rituals over the years. All of them promising numinous powers or gifts to the one who followed their instructions. She hadn't immediately run out and wrapped herself in coyote skins or ingested moldy mushrooms in any of those cases.

And yet she couldn't help but feel that she was standing on the edge of a precipice. The slightest move to the right or left could see her tumbling madly into the unknown.

Sheridan would laugh her fool head off.

Meru nodded to herself. "I'm being naïve again, letting my wild imagination get the better of me."

She stilled and pulled in a deep breath, trying to calm her racing pulse.

Her eyes fell on her notebook once again. "Oh, what the heck?"

She found herself in front of her window once more, listening to the resonant chanting below. Her heart pounded a drumbeat to match. Flinging her head back dramatically, fully prepared to feel ridiculous, she read aloud.

I lift the veil behind which lies
Secrets shielded from my eyes
All Others by their Magick hidden
Are from my sight no more forbidden
Awaken mind where true eye dwells

Awaken soul within your shell
I call to Danu in my plight
Illuminate this darkest night

Light flashed before her eyes as a strange heatlike sensation flooded her limbs. The room began to spin, light brightening to a blinding level until everything went black.

Just as the clock struck midnight.

* * * * *

She was standing beside a river near a green hill or mound, like the ones she'd seen in pictures of Ireland. And she wasn't alone. There was a woman off in the distance. She was gesturing to Meru and she seemed to be speaking.

Be careful, now. Danger.

But how could there be danger in such a beautiful place? No sooner had the thought formed than the scene changed. She was running. Running through the woods, chased by something that she couldn't see but still managed to send chills through to her bones.

Run!

Ahead of her, a giant black wolflike beast came charging. She was sure she was about to die when it leapt over her head and attacked the darkness that pursued her.

The shadows and the feeling of foreboding disappeared as her savior turned to look her way. The wolf-beast morphed into the gloriously naked figure of a man. Her heart raced, breathless as he began to slowly stalk her.

She couldn't see him clearly, but she felt the carnal hunger rolling off him in waves, his steps purposeful as he closed the distance between them. He was tall, impossibly tall, shoulders broad, muscles rippling with power, gleaming in the shadowy light of the forest.

Molten need coiled low in her belly and her limbs trembled with a sudden overwhelming desire, not to flee, but to submit.

She strained to study the details of his face, only catching a glimpse of dark hair and glowing eyes before he reached for her shoulders and turned her away from him. He pulled her back against the burning heat of his belly, his hair-roughened chest abrading her back as his jutting cock pressed hard against her flesh.

His hot breath sent a scalding path of fire down her neck as he inhaled her scent. A low pleasure-filled growl emerged from his chest and sent delicious chills over her skin, causing her breasts to swell and tighten in anticipation. Her nipples peaked, reaching, aching for his touch. Her limbs trembled, shudders racking her as she tried to contain the hot sensations. She panted as this strange need rose to a fever pitch, breathing deeply of his scent and the dark aroma of the forest around them.

A part of her wondered that she had no fear of this stranger, this wolf. He cupped her aching breasts in his calloused palms, caressing them as his blunt fingers pinched and tugged at her nipples. Her body arched under the stinging lash of sensation, his heat, his strength and scent surrounding her. She closed her eyes and rolled her head back against him, unable to consider fear in the face of the intense yearning that seemed to overtake her at his touch.

She moaned in protest when those hands left her breasts to grip her shoulders. He pressed down and she knew instinctively what he wanted.

More than happy to comply, near senseless with lust, she knelt on the cool, moss-covered ground. The earthy green scent filled her lungs, her breathing fast and shallow as she waited for what would come next. Anticipation made her stomach clench and her body shake as goose bumps broke over her flesh.

He covered her smaller form, her rounded curves seeming dainty and fragile beneath his massive frame. His hot skin pressed against her thighs, the friction feeding her rising desire. Her fingers dug into the soft ground and she pushed her hips back against his pulsing cock.

He groaned but gripped her hips in warning. Then she was gasping as his rough, broad tongue stroked down her sweat-dampened spine, seeming to savor her taste.

His head lowered and she stilled. His questing tongue swiped one curving cheek, then the next, before dipping lower, licking at thighs already coated with cream. She arched her neck on a cry of hot desperation as he growled against her swollen sex. Her pussy clenched on nothing as he caught the drops of moisture with his tongue, nipping at her clit, and she moaned, muscles locking tight.

"Sweet." She heard the raspy, nearly unintelligible word moments before pleasure blocked out all coherent thought. She fell onto her elbows, her forehead pressed to the damp earth, as her dream lover pressed her thighs further apart, spreading her wide for his inspection.

She whimpered, excitement whipping through her. *Yes. Oh yes.* This was what she wanted, what she needed.

"*Mine.*"

Her breath caught at the fierce possession in his deep voice, and she closed her eyes, waiting, knowing he would claim her. Her body jerked as his lips wrapped around her clit, his tongue lapping teasingly. Every cell in her body focused on the man behind her, willing him to finish what he started. She'd never imagined wanting anything as much as she wanted this man, this *wolf*, at this moment.

He rose up behind her and she felt the thick head of his cock against her soaking entrance. It slid against the lips of her pussy, teasing her with a need she could barely fathom.

"Please." She heard the breathless plea and realized it came from her. She didn't care. She was so close…

Meru woke up facedown on the floor in her living room, moaning and choking on a loose bit of fluff from the throw rug. She was soaked with sweat, desperate and aroused.

Pulling herself up, she showered and dressed as quickly as her shaky limbs would allow. Sexual frustration and confusion swamped her. She'd never fainted in her life. Growing up with Sheridan, the "gross out" tomboy, that was saying something.

And that dream. She would be the first to admit she had a rich fantasy life. But never had a dream been that vivid...that primal. Her sexual fantasies usually included silk sheets and candlelight, a far cry from kneeling with her knees in the dirt, begging for the rough ministrations of a stranger. A werewolf, no less.

The mysterious book lay closed on the floor where she'd left it last night. Unwilling to leave it behind, she placed it in her old backpack and made the short walk to the professor's house in record time.

No one was home. Feeling moderately defeated, she decided to stop at the corner diner for a late birthday breakfast.

In line to pick up her order, she noticed it. *The glow.*

She rubbed her eyes but it was still there. Everyone in line, all the people in the diner were surrounded by an outline of white light, pulsing with life.

But beyond that, each person was different. There were shades of violet and aqua blue, countless colors varying only in strength and brightness. The impatient man in the business suit just in front of her had a cloud of angry red vibrating around his head as he argued on his cell phone. The young girl at the checkout counter was cloaked in bubble gum pink as she flirted with the man on the stool near the cash register.

She recalled a book on auras she'd seen only yesterday at Aunt Lily's shop. *Is that what I'm seeing?*

Combined with the fainting episode, she was seriously considering the possibility of a brain tumor when her eyes landed on a vision that stopped her heart cold. It was the man Miss Bubble Gum was chatting up. At first glance, he seemed like an ordinary, even handsome man in his mid-twenties. He couldn't have been more normal.

Apart from the forked tongue, scales and slanted yellow eyes.

He spoke to the cashier, who didn't seem to notice that she was batting her eyes at something that looked like it had escaped from a bad alien invasion miniseries. And then he caught Meru staring. He smiled charmingly around sharp, pointy teeth but grew still as he noted her horrified expression. He looked around at the crowded restaurant before catching her eye once more...and winking.

She flew out of there as if the hounds of Hell were on her heels. For all she knew, they might have been. She slowed near The Knot, trying to convince herself that what she'd seen was a costume or extensive plastic surgery. This was Montrose after all, home to Houston's free spirits, artists and all things strange and unusual.

Her gaze focused curiously on the people milling around her. Interspersed throughout the still glimmering throng of humanity, she saw *them*.

A pair of lovely Elvin creatures, who looked as if they'd bathed in a shower of gold, traversed the crosswalk just ahead.

A man dressed in overalls who, calm as you please, shifted into a panther as he rounded the corner.

And here and there, hiding in the shadows as they attempted to avoid the others, several more of those lizard men slithered.

It had worked. That ridiculous spell had actually worked! That was the only explanation. "The Veil" had lifted and apparently, the other side was a lot closer than she'd ever imagined.

She wasn't sure she'd ever go outside again.

*****

"You say that sweet Professor White gave you this book?" At her nod, Lily's lips pursed and she seemed to look inward for an answer.

She'd come over right away after Meru's panicked call and now her reassuring presence on the couch and the warm clasp of her hand were finally taking some of the chill out of Meru's bones.

Meru gasped softly as she saw the energy around her aunt coalesce into the rose-colored outline of another woman. Sitting on the floor right beside her.

Meru reached out her hand to the new energy and felt a rush of warmth and love. A tear fell unheeded down her cheek. Lily looked at her niece and began to tear up as well.

"Is that—" Meru's voice trembled.

At Lily's nod, she began sobbing softly. Lily took her in her arms, rocking her until she quieted. "It's okay, love. Seeing one's mother again after she's been dead for twenty-six years is a lot to take in. When Rose first starting speaking to me and entering my dreams, even *I* was a bit overwhelmed."

Lily set her away and pulled something from her bag.

"I knew this was the perfect time for me to give you your present," she said forcefully, smiling brightly through her own tears.

It was a square, flat jewelry box. Meru lifted the lid and gasped. A thin, intricately carved bronze torc lay on the dark velvet.

"This has been handed down to every firstborn female in our family for as long as anyone can remember. It belonged to my mother. And then Rose. And now…it belongs to you." She lovingly placed the braided metal around Meru's neck. "Professor White gave you a very special gift and helped to unlock what was already within you. This is your mother's gift to you. She said it was time for you to have it."

Meru looked at the open ends of the Celtic heirloom, touching the carved heads with wonder. "Wolves?"

Lily rubbed her back and nodded. "Your great-grandmother used to tell us that our ancestors were great Druids and that their totem, their animal protector, was the wolf. It guided them and kept them safe."

A sad glimmer passed through her eyes as she continued and Meru knew her aunt was thinking of the tragic car accident that had taken her sister.

"It can't protect you from all things, but it will always protect your spirit from the darkness." Lily chuckled self-consciously. "At least, that's what Grams used to say."

With that, she stood and led Meru into her small bedroom, heading for her clothes closet with a determined step.

"Now, we aren't going to think about anything more today except what you're wearing tonight. I believe Sheridan said something about that lovely blue dress. I can't wait to finally see you in it."

"But I—"

"No arguments, young lady." She pulled out the shimmering midnight blue material and tossed it on the bed before walking to the phone. "Tomorrow, you and I will camp out on that secretive professor's lawn if we have to. Trust me, love, I want to see him just as much as you do. But today is your birthday, a day of possibilities, so I say just try to enjoy it."

Meru gasped and stared at her aunt. She'd repeated Professor White's words nearly verbatim.

"I mean it," Lily affirmed forcefully. "The gift of sight you've been given…well, it's just that. A gift." She cradled the phone to her ear and began to dial. "Now we'll order a birthday pizza and do your nails. That dress definitely calls for a French manicure."

Chapter Two

"If you need...*anything*..." The giggling cocktail waitress leaned over, showing her ample cleavage as if to emphasize her words. "Anything at all, I'll be right over there."

Never one to ignore such a tempting offer, Finn purred back, "Thank you, Candy. I'll be sure to call on you when it's time to...satisfy my sweet tooth."

Damon raised his brow before nudging Finn with his elbow. "Knock it off. We're here on business."

The auburn-haired Fae took his eyes off the young server, releasing her from his mesmerizing glance.

"Just trying to have a little fun, that's all. Letting off some steam after being trapped in that parking lot masquerading as an expressway for the last hour. Why that thrilling escapade was necessary, I'll never know. Hey, Val—trade me."

He reached across the table, grabbing the greasy paper boat filled with fries from the large blond man who was simultaneously swiping Finn's cheeseburger with an agreeable nod.

"Myrddin's orders were clear. No Magick." Damon ran a hand through his dark hair, scanning the crowded bar-and-grill, his shoulders tense. "That's why we had to get in that damn death trap of a rental car in the first place. We have to stay under the radar for now."

He smiled a bit as Finn mumbled under his breath and jammed a French fry into his mouth. It galled his friend to have to rein in his abilities. Finn had never been one to follow the rules. He simply felt they didn't apply to him. And being such a powerful Fae creature, a member of a noble house of the Tuatha Dé Danann no less, for the most part he was right.

Damon and Val had at least been regular mortals once, though granted, they had each seen a millennium come and go since then. Actually Damon had seen closer to four, but who was counting? They could still vaguely remember the frustration of actually working for what you wanted as opposed to the instant gratification Finn had been weaned on.

"Why are we here again?" Val wondered aloud, taking a large bite into his burger, groaning his enjoyment as if it had been months instead of mere hours since they'd last eaten.

Finn looked up with a wink. "Cause somebody 'messed with Texas'?"

Damon rolled his eyes. "You heard Myrddin this afternoon. There's been a lot of *Dark* in the area. Their activity is increasing for some reason. More than just the usual insanity that pops up around this time of year. According to him, they seem to be looking for something."

"Or someone." Val added, tilting his head in thought as he swallowed. "He was suspiciously vague about that, wasn't he? I mean, he said he'd tell us everything tomorrow but he kept sending Dragon Boy dirty looks after he shot his mouth off about that priestess."

Damon had noticed that too. The Shambhalan, or Dragon Boy as Val tended to call him, had mentioned something about the safety of the priestess and the elder had swiftly silenced him. All he had told them was that very serious powers were at play here and he needed the *Fianna* and their "unique" skills to handle the situation.

For Damon, there was no question of his allegiance. If the old man hadn't found him and taken him in, showing him how to control his abilities, how to deal with his anger, well, there was no telling what kind of monster he would have become.

They all owed Myrddin in one way or another, which was how they'd ended up as *Fianna*, the guardians of the North Portal. They were often the only thing standing between unaware humans and the *Dark*, the name long ago given to the various shifters and supernatural servants of their enemies. The *Dark* were ruled by those on the other side of the portal who sought dominion over humanity.

Myrddin, Damon had learned not long after their initial meeting, was himself an Archon, one of the advanced beings from beyond the portal. When they'd first arrived in Earth's dimension, he and many of the others were believed to be gods.

Time and tragedy had shown most Archons the potential of the human race, potential *their* presence seemed to stifle. A council was formed and the decision to leave the Earth and its inhabitants to their own devices was unanimous.

Well, nearly unanimous.

A few, less enlightened Archons, those who controlled the *Dark*, believed their superior technological and magickal abilities gave them the right to enslave the weaker race. Those Archons became criminals in their own dimension...and a deadly threat to humanity's.

From that moment on the four entry points, or portals from their dimension to Earth's, were guarded against encroachment from either side. But that didn't seem to stop the *Dark* from finding their way through and that was where the *Fianna*, as well as a few select Others, came in.

His position on the council prevented Myrddin from taking direct action, but he aided Damon and his team with information and advice whenever he could, often bending the rules he wasn't allowed to break. The Archon's noninterference dictates often put Myrddin at odds with his own people. Still, the wily Elder always found a loophole with which to protect himself and the *Fianna*.

Perhaps that was why the direct call for assistance so far from their home base had thrown Damon and his men. Why were the *Dark* descending en masse on a city so far from any of the portals? Why call the northern guardians instead of requesting the aid of those more familiar with the area?

And who had the Shambhalan been referring to when he'd mentioned the priestess?

"Frankly," Finn interrupted Damon's somber musings, "I don't care where we fight the baddies—the end result will be the same. Besides, I think a change of pace will do us all some good. And this place is certainly different. Hot as the Netherworld...but different."

Damon had to agree. He missed the cool, green forests of home. Why in the name of the gods had the Elder brought them here? And why had he sent them to this bar, The Blue Easy? The most dangerous thing that he could see here were the burgers. Maybe the group of rowdy college kids playing pool on the other side of the bar.

No, they were nothing that would warrant *Fianna* attention.

Above the band and the noises of the crowd, he heard a chorus of happy voices raise in greeting. They started to sing. It was someone's birthday. He sighed, immediately feeling as if he'd been sucker-punched.

Her. He'd come for her.

He sensed her before he saw her. Caught her distinct scent despite the mass of heated bodies, the thick smoke and heavy perfume that hovered in the air. Summer fields of lavender and exotic spice.

Mine.

Shocked by his own thoughts he stood, scanning the throng intently in search of the source of that delicious aroma.

There. Surrounded by her friends, reluctantly allowing herself to be pulled up on stage to join the band. It was obvious they knew her, and judging by the loud response from the crowd, they weren't the only ones. She was stunning, curvaceous...luscious.

Mine, the voice inside him roared determinedly. The people grew quiet as she began to sing an old, familiar blues song. Her voice was pure and raw, all smoke and heat, heartbreak and sex. It gripped his cock in a velvet fist and his heart pounded hard to the sensual rhythm.

He watched as her full lips wrapped around the mournful notes, his mind racing with images of her spread out beneath him, those lush lips pressed against his own, open and gasping as he spread her soft, creamy thighs and thrust into her waiting—

Shifting slightly at his body's instinctive answer to her siren call, Damon bumped into the smirking Finn, who'd come to stand beside him, along with Val. Damned Tuatha and their telepathic abilities. He bristled. It was obvious Finn was aware of his thoughts and just as obvious that his friend wouldn't be able to hold his tongue.

"She is incredible, isn't she?" Finn waggled his elegant brow. "Not only a voice that would tempt a saint, but that body! For such a tiny little thing, she has got one amazing pair of—"

A low, threatening growl interrupted his words. No one was more stunned than Damon to find out it was actually coming from him.

"Calm down, Damon." Val placed a hand on his shoulder, whether for comfort or restraint, Damon wasn't sure. "Finn is just trying to rile you. We're here to do a job for—"

"Me. You're here to do a job for me. And you're late."

Damon looked down at the tall, slender woman in the skimpy red halter and low-rise jeans. Her braided hair fell over her shoulder almost to her waist, drawing his eyes momentarily to the jeweled ring twinkling at her navel. His gaze immediately returned to the stage, throat tight with need for the small woman shining beneath the spotlight.

The aggressive newcomer would not be ignored. She grabbed his hand in a surprisingly firm grip, doing the same with Finn and Val in turn as she introduced herself. "Sheridan Kelly. And you three must be from the agency. I have to tell y'all, they really outdid themselves this time. You guys are *hot!*"

Finn refused to release her hand, crowding closer to her, the instinctive Fae sensuality emanating from every pore. "Sheridan Kelly, the pleasure is all mine."

Damon watched from the corner of his eye as she was snared by his friend's purple-hued gaze for a breathless heartbeat before stepping back, tugging her hand out of Finn's and crossing her arms defensively.

"Save it, Pretty Boy, I didn't hire you for me. Nice colored contacts, though. A real fashion statement. Come to think of it, I only asked Martha to send one of you stud muffins. If she thinks I'm paying for three—" She paused in thought. "Actually, this might be a good thing. She'll never suspect until it's too late."

Val raised his hand a bit sheepishly. "I'm confused."

The woman looked him up and down and sighed, biting her lip in a way that had Finn shifting restlessly. Damon grinned. Finn hated being ignored.

"Too bad it isn't *my* birthday. With that hair and that bod, you look exactly like Brad…only bigger."

Damon huffed under his breath, amused, even as he was frustrated by her distraction.

Val shrugged in apology and she laughed in disbelief. "Seriously? Don't they have movie theaters where you're from? Brad? The actor? Nothing?" She shook her head as his expression remained puzzled.

"Okay, here's the deal. See that woman onstage?"

For the first time since she'd arrived, she had Damon's full attention.

"Well, that's my cousin Meru and today is her birthday. She's expecting me to do something crazy, and of course I will, but I need to throw her off a bit first. She's been acting weird tonight anyway, so it shouldn't be a problem."

They all stared at her blankly.

She rolled her eyes. "Geesh, I told Martha I needed brawn *and* brains."

Finn visibly flinched at the insult but said nothing.

"Listen carefully." She drew out her words, her eyes mocking. "You will come to our table. I'll introduce you as friends of mine from the fire department. One of you will have to be Bob, since I already told her about him. You'll have a few drinks...on me of course. Try to contribute a bit of interesting conversation if you can. And then, when she's confident I haven't done anything more embarrassing than trying to set her up on another blind date...you'll do what I hired you to do."

"Which is?" Finn asked stiffly. Sheridan's eyes widened in surprise.

"Why, strip, of course."

While they all stared at her with their mouths open, she started to turn and then paused, one eyebrow raised in cocky warning. "Oh, and by the way, I'm a cop, so be careful where you put your hands. I'd hate to haul anyone in tonight."

They looked at each other as she stalked away.

"She can't be serious." Val's deep brown eyes flickered momentarily to eerie amber, indicating his feelings about the turn this night had taken.

Finn laughed without humor. "Oh, she was quite serious.

Damon tore his gaze from the stage once more to grin at his friend's consternation. In all these long years, Finn had yet to meet a female immune to his wiles. Human, Fae or *Dark*, there were none that could resist him ...until now.

He glared at Damon. "Laugh it up, my friend, but I say something is seriously wrong with that girl." He lowered his voice and sounded a little mystified. "I couldn't read her at all."

Val's jaw dropped. "Wow. Has that ever—"

"No, never," Finn affirmed. "Mark my words, that Sheridan Kelly is dangerous." His eyes flew to the table they were supposed to approach casually in a few minutes and he smiled wickedly.

"Her cousin, on the other hand, looks like a lovely handful. Just call me Bob."

Damon's low rumble of displeasure caused Val to step closer, his body tensing, his expression one of concern. "Okay, okay, you can be Bob! Get a grip, man. Damn, you boys are acting strange tonight."

He watched as Val scanned the crowd once more "Are you sure we should be going along with this? I mean, Myrddin sent us here for a reason. I don't think it was to put ourselves on display for a group of slavering females."

"How do you know?" Finn asked innocently. "The old man *has* always had a really bizarre sense of humor."

Damon ended the debate without a word. She was stepping off the stage and out of his view, which was unacceptable. His six-foot-five-inch frame came in handy now, parting the crowd effortlessly as he strode toward the source of his new obsession.

Meru. He mouthed her name silently as he closed in on her table. It felt right on his tongue.

Would the rest of her taste as sweet?

Meru walked off the stage with a distracted smile for the people clapping and calling out congratulations. She hadn't seen the musicians for a while and it was fun to jam again after so many years. Her heart just wasn't in it tonight.

She made a beeline for the table and swallowed down a large gulp of the fruity mixed drink Sheridan had ordered for her. A few more of these and maybe she'd be able to pretend that this hadn't been the strangest day of her life.

Since this afternoon she'd been abandoned by her aunt, who'd said she had an important errand to run. She'd then been, for all intents and purposes, kidnapped by her pushy cousin for a night on the town. And it wasn't over yet. If she knew Sheridan, and she did, the brat had something up her sleeve.

Her only recourse seemed to be getting quietly drunk in her favorite bar, surrounded by her *glowing* friends and trying very hard not to scan the area for Lizards and other assorted creatures that had once been safely relegated to nightmares and fairytales. Frankly, she was surprised she was taking it so well.

When she thought about it, though, it seemed almost as if she had been preparing for it her whole life. Her very own thesis had, before she'd shredded it, postulated that myth, even fantastic myth, could have actual basis in fact.

She grinned foolishly into her drink. If only the department heads at the university could see what she'd seen today. Honestly, she didn't think anything, no matter how strange or mysterious, could surprise her after this.

Except, of course, whether or not her overly endowed body was going to stay in this travesty of a dress her aunt had squeezed her into. She attempted to tug the front up to a decent level, uncomfortably aware of how much skin she'd been revealing to the crowded bar. All she managed to accomplish was a whole lot of jiggling flesh and no new coverage.

She was tempted to try again when a heartfelt, decidedly tortured male groan froze her fingers mid motion.

Three of the sexiest men she'd ever seen were standing beside her table.

Meru, you are the queen of understatement, the voice inside her head let out a low, rather vulgar wolf whistle. Before she got the chance to speak, let alone find the owner of the husky sound that had caught her attention, Sheridan appeared, her partner Kyle in tow.

"Finally," she said in an annoyed tone to the tense-looking men beside her. "Meru, these are the guys I was telling you about. From the firehouse?"

Then she looked at them and hesitated. The largest, and sexiest of the lot in Meru's opinion, took a quick step forward. Sheridan nodded in apparent approval and turned back to Meru.

"This is Bob." Her cousin couldn't have looked more pleased with herself.

Meru's eyes widened in surprise. "He doesn't look like a Bob."

Sheridan let out a put-upon sigh. "What do you mean he doesn't look like a Bob? He is, okay? He is a Bob. And these are his friends..." She seemed to be struggling to remember the names of everyone, but they beat her to the punch.

"My name is Finn," The obvious charmer of the group smiled gently into her eyes. "This is Val. You've already met our man, Bob." He chuckled at the black glare he received from his giant friend in response.

"And you, my dear," he continued, "are the rightfully praised cousin Meru. You have a beautiful singing voice, by the way." She nodded her thanks as she stared at him suspiciously.

Meru tried not to "look" at them, she just couldn't help it. A sigh of relief escaped when she realized that none of them were Lizards. Oddly, she felt no fear, only fascination. Maybe it was that pep talk she'd had with Lily. Or maybe it was the sheer sexual pheromones they all seemed to be emitting with each breath.

Whatever the case, Meru sensed that none of these "men" were a danger to her physical well being. Quite the contrary, in fact.

The man called Finn was stunning, in a totally *not human* way. Tall, lean and elegantly muscled, with aristocratic features, short mahogany-colored hair and unbelievably lovely eyes. He glimmered like starlight. The energy he generated was not an aura around him, but *in* him, under the skin.

The one he'd introduced as Val was a giant mass of golden muscle. The faded logo of a popular heavy metal band stretched across the broad expanse of his black t-shirt, and his snug black jeans clung to thighs the size of small tree trunks. He looked like he'd be more at home in leather and fur. With his shoulder-length dark blond hair and features that made him almost too good-looking, he reminded Meru of that movie star Sheridan was always going on about...only bigger.

He smiled at her, a surprisingly friendly, open grin, as if inviting her to laugh with him.

She looked at the tattoo of a hawk in flight bursting from his left biceps and watched it pulse with a life all its own. She couldn't contain her gasp at the sight.

"What's wrong?" The rich, gravelly voice had her thighs squeezing together, her body shivering in appreciation.

Bob.

He had to be over six and a half feet in height, his shoulders so wide they nearly blocked out the bandstand behind him.

This man, dark and sinfully masculine, made her breath catch and other parts of her she was trying desperately to ignore clench and tighten with a sudden, astonishing desire. She'd never experienced anything like it. At least, not while she was awake.

He too was dressed all in black from head to toe, making her think a bit giddily that it must be the standard uniform for hot, hunky Others. He was a sight to make a grown woman weep.

And he looked oddly familiar.

She felt the rush of power, of untamed earthiness pulsing around him, reaching out to wrap around her. Everything about him made her logical mind scream *"Danger!"*, though her feminine instincts were dancing for joy as they continued to catalogue his lust-inducing features.

Thick hair the color of a raven's wing fell carelessly forward over his brow and his brooding, sensual eyes were black and intense. They focused on her with unswerving intent.

Bob was a Greek god.

That was the only possible explanation. And he had to be a jerk, she thought hazily. No one could possibly look this good and be a nice guy to boot. Her instincts disagreed but she wasn't completely convinced they were thinking any clearer than she was at the moment.

She felt his gaze as a physical caress and realized her body had been unconsciously leaning toward him, drawn by the magnetic pull. She unclenched her hands and reached up to fiddle with one of the small, carved heads of her mother's torc. His eyes followed the movement and widened in surprise…and she knew.

Meru turned to glare at her cousin. "How did you meet these guys?"

Sheridan looked startled and tried to act affronted. "I told you! They're—"

"They are *not* firemen. They are something else entirely."

Sheridan stuttered out a nervous laugh. "Well, what do you think they are? Strippers or something?"

"No." Meru rolled her eyes and stood a little unsteadily, pointing at each man in turn. "This guy is Fae."

Kyle looked at Sheridan in confusion. "He said his name was Finn."

Meru sighed heavily. "His *name* is Finn, Kyle, but he *is* a Fae. As in Fae folk? Faeries? Ringing any bells?"

Finn's lavender eyes went impossibly wide only to narrow dangerously when Sheridan muttered, "Well, I did say he was a pretty boy."

Meru turned to Damon. "Bob here, who by the way in no way, shape, or form *looks* like a Bob. Not that I have anything against that name, mind you." Meru realized she was babbling.

"*Bob* is a sexy Wolf." Then Val. "And he—well—he's...well, there's *two* of him!"

Val swore under his breath, but Bob's dark eyes latched onto hers and twinkled.

"You think I'm sexy?"

That voice again. Her knees suddenly turned to jelly. Her cousin's arm around her shoulder thankfully kept her upright.

"It's all right, hon, I've gotcha." She said in an overly sweet tone. "How many drinks have you had today, Cuz?" Sheridan looked at the men apologetically. "She's usually much more coherent. Maybe it's the trauma of facing old age."

Meru pulled away from her cousin indignantly, only to lose her balance, already precarious because of the sadistic high heels that went with her sorry excuse for a dress. She wobbled dangerously before two bands of steel masquerading as arms wrapped around her waist.

The heat from his body was overwhelming. She blushed and kept her eyes glued to a button on his shirt as she felt her breasts brushed against his muscled torso. A purely feminine shiver overtook her as he pulled her more fully against him. He was hard all over, a mountain of solid muscle. Standing this close, she felt like a child beside him, but how his nearness affected her was in no way innocent.

So she apparently had a thing for wolves. *Go figure.* She felt his arms tighten instinctively around her before he slowly withdrew his support. It was almost as if he was savoring the contact, was as affected as she by their sudden attraction.

"You're right, you know."

Her eyes returned to his at his words and he threw a lethal half smile in her direction.

"My name isn't really Bob. It's Damon. Damon Arkadios." He reached out and, though his grasp on her fingers couldn't have been gentler, his expressive eyes gleamed with fierce determination.

"Dance with me."

Ignoring the stunned expressions on Val and Finn's faces, as well as the sputtering from her cousin, Damon pulled a dazed-looking Meru with him onto the small, crowded dance floor while the band played yet another sultry tune.

He didn't dance. Couldn't in his long memory recall the last time he'd even tried. He did not court or woo or romance. He was no Finn, after all. He was a warrior, a Guardian. More than that...

And worse than that, he grimaced. On those rare occasions when he couldn't control his needs or was unwilling to handle the situation himself, he found a Fae or Shifter female. He needed someone strong enough in their Magick and experienced enough to handle the wild nature of his beast's sexuality.

He was *not* a gentle man. But he wanted to be gentle with her. He just couldn't seem to stop himself from holding her again. She felt too right in his arms. And that scared him as nothing else ever could because there were reasons he should be wary. There was her strange knowledge of what they were, the danger in this area and the fact that she was a small and fragile human.

But in spite of all that, he couldn't quite convince himself to let her go yet.

His large hands easily spanned her waist and he pulled her closer, a growl of need threatening to break free as he felt her body pressing against his own once more, her arms rising hesitantly toward his shoulders.

She felt so small beside him, and her elfin face, with its deep blue eyes and those delectable freckles sprinkled across her nose, implied an innocence and fragility that both drew and terrified him. He had the odd desire to kiss each cocoa-colored spot in turn.

His gaze was drawn to her lips. They were a sensual contradiction to the youthful purity that marked the rest of her features. A full and utterly edible temptation.

Her body...Well, that was sin itself. Curvaceous and lush, with full, soft breasts and gently rounded hips, it was the promise of a hot, silken haven to a rough warrior. He lowered his hands to grasp those perfect hips and pressed himself against her, lost to sensation.

A fine tremor ran through her small frame and her nipples hardened into sharp little points that taunted him through the fabric of their clothes. *Fear or desire?*

He bent to inhale deeply, pressing his lips against the curve of her neck. The answering aroma washed over him in rich waves. He shuddered and the wolf deep within shouted his triumph. She wanted him.

The scent of her need was intoxicating. He wanted to wallow in it, wanted to cover her in his own. To mark her as his in the most elemental, primal way possible.

He'd been controlling his inner demon for millennia but it took every bit of willpower he possessed to rein in his lust for the tiny female in his arms.

Meru took a deep breath. Then another. Trying to think had just become a tall order. What woman could when the object of her hottest fantasy was nibbling on her neck? Never in her life had she been so aroused, so hyperaware of another.

She pressed closer instinctively, stilling as she came into contact with the proof of his arousal. The unbelievably, impossibly large proof. No one was actually that...blessed, she thought in disbelief.

But he isn't human, is he? At least, not completely. The logic of her inner voice couldn't be refuted. It gave her the distance she needed to lean back in the circle of his arms, away from the temptation of his lips and look into his eyes.

Big mistake. She was immediately entranced by the irresistible combination of lust and bemusement in his expression, probably identical to the look in her own. Her mind raced desperately for a way to break the spell before she thoroughly humiliated herself by raping the poor man in front of all and sundry.

"So, not Bob?" Oh, clever girl. Apparently all those years in college hadn't included a class in witty repartee with a sexy wolf-man.

His eyes homed in on her lips as she spoke, causing her to lick them nervously.

"No," he rasped.

"Not a fireman?" She felt the light graze of fingers caressing the hollow of her neck where her pulse raced madly.

"No."

"Werewolf?" she squeaked softly as his roaming touch reached her low neckline, her shallow breaths pushing the upper swell of her breasts against his hand as if in invitation. His dark lashes shielded his eyes as he hesitated momentarily.

"No." He corrected slowly. "Lycan."

Her brow furrowed in confusion. "What's the difference?"

"It's complicated." He muttered without elaboration.

Okay, doesn't like to talk about himself, she noted, her brain scrambling for an alternate topic.

"Where did you meet Sheridan?" She was stunned by the slight taint of jealousy in her tone. She had never been jealous of Sheridan. Oh sure, she'd often grumped at the fates that had gifted her cousin with all the grace, all the height *and* the ability to tan instead of burn. Not to mention an outgoing, confident nature. But that wasn't Sher's fault. It was just the way the genes were doled out.

Meru had long ago come to terms with being short, pale and pleasantly plump. The only person who'd ever made her feel bad about her weight was her ex. And he was history.

Damon chuckled softly, the sound grabbing her attention and causing an unexpected throb in her womb, heat coiling low in her belly. His nostrils flared, as if he could smell her increasing desire.

He jerked his dark eyes to hers. The hand that had stilled began moving again, the backs of his fingers caressing the flesh above her dress. His grip on her hip firmed, pulling her lower body snugly against his once more as he answered.

"I just met her a few moments ago." he assured her. His broad shoulders shielded her from curious eyes as his fingers slid just beneath the blue fabric. The rough tips grazing the bare, sensitive points of her breasts caused her to gasp quietly, and she felt Damon's body respond with an answering pulse of excitement against her soft belly.

Her eyes narrowed and he removed the tempting digits to her safer, albeit still sensitive, neckline. She shifted her hips away in an attempt to concentrate on his words instead of his touch, but she didn't even think of stopping him.

Something didn't add up. She peered around his massive arm to look distractedly at her cousin, who appeared to be arguing vehemently with Kyle and a...well, a half-naked fireman. Finn watched the man through narrowed eyes, while Val was apparently too busy fending off the gaggle of women who had converged around their table since his arrival, to notice. Who could blame them?

The fireman was obviously a stripper. A stripper Sheridan was trying, without much success, to send home before he started a riot. From his stubborn expression, it seemed he took his commitments very seriously. He slipped off his shiny yellow coat and nodded to the band. The crowd went wild as he began to gyrate against the flustered Sheridan while the lead singer started wailing about love giving him a fever.

Finn stood and stared the man down. The fireman swallowed, raising his hands as if in surrender, leaving Sheridan and moving on to the happy crowd of females waving dollar bills.

The light bulb in her fruity drink muddled head turned on. That must be Bob. The *real* Bob.

Meru looked back at Damon, who hadn't been paying any attention to the unfolding drama, too fascinated with her cleavage to look away.

"She hired strippers again, didn't she? And she thought you—"

Damon blushed and she laughed outright. An indignant look came over his face at the sound.

"You don't think I could do it?" He tried to sound offended, though he was obviously fighting a smile.

She rolled her eyes, still chortling. "I have no doubt that someone who looked like you would be a millionaire inside a week."

His expression turned feral and he leaned down, rubbing her cheek with his as he whispered, "Oh, that's right. You think I'm sexy." She could actually feel her bones dissolve as he growled softly in her ear.

Forgetting where she was, the fact that she barely knew him or that she didn't do things like this, she responded instinctively. She bit him. Gently placed one sexy lobe between her teeth…and licked.

At any other time, she would have been mortified by her own actions. She supposed she could blame it on her strange day or the cocktails but it wouldn't be the truth. It was all him.

They had stopped dancing. Every muscle in his body trembled with restraint. She turned her head slightly to catch his eye and inhaled sharply at the look of concentrated need on his face.

Blazing eyes focused on her mouth with obvious intent. He leaned closer, close enough that she could feel his breath against her lips. She had never wanted anyone to kiss her so badly in her entire life.

Sheridan's voice hit her like a bucket of ice water. "You and me. Ladies' room. Now." She was ripped away, and none to gently, as her cousin strong armed her off the dance floor. She looked over her shoulder helplessly to see Finn and Val talking to Damon.

He didn't look happy.

Through the red haze that seemed to surrounded him, Damon heard Finn and Val calling his name.

"Snap out of it, *faol.*" Finn whispered harshly. "You're drawing unwanted attention."

Damon looked down at his rippling fists, battling his need to grab his mate and carry her away from any interference.

My mate? The thought shocked him back into himself. He'd never felt so untamed, so out of control. It was her fault. *Meru.* He'd been fine, seriously turned on, but fine—until she'd bitten him. And then that cousin of hers had ripped her away. He'd almost shifted on the spot.

He breathed deeply to regain control. That was when he sensed them. He almost hadn't recognized the scent at first. It had been a long time since they'd last surfaced.

He signaled the others with a subtle motion of his hand and they immediately backed off, spreading out as casually as possible to search. Later he would castigate himself for his dangerous distraction but not now. It was time to hunt.

As they stood in line in the ladies' room, Meru listened to Sheridan's relentless lecture on the evils of drinking and biting strange men.

So did the six other girls crammed into the smallish space with them.

From the looks on their faces, they thought her cousin was as crazy as she did. They must have seen the buff god she was dancing with.

"I really don't think you have any room to talk here, Sher. I mean, you're the one who thought he was that stripper."

"But that's just it, Meru. Why didn't they correct my mistake? They just...went along. Who would do that?"

The girls in line looked at each other with eyebrows raised at Sheridan's question. *Men on the make*, their expressions seem to say.

"You don't need to hook up with a liar, no matter how pretty the package. I know the perfect—"

"Oh no you don't, Sher." Meru had to interrupt. "You no longer have the blind date trust. Remember Howard Delaney? Howard 'The Nose'? Enough said."

"Hey, he's working on the sneezing thing. Just because he still lives with his mother—"

"Forget it. I think I'm doing okay on my own."

Her fellow line-mates nodded in agreement. Meru noticed a few of them eyeing the door and she just knew they were wondering if they could have a go at her dance partner. The stripper had scared all the decent men away and the pickings *were* getting slim. She had seen enough.

When it was Sheridan's turn in the stall, she made an impulsive decision.

Gesturing to the other girls, she put a finger to her lips. They all nodded, giant grins on their faces, as she slipped out the door and stepped into the narrow hallway that led back to the bar. Today was still her birthday. Meru wanted to be kissed.

She looked down, trying to avoid tripping over a fallen beer bottle, and found herself bumping head first into a passerby. Glancing up, a smile of apology on her lips, she paled.

"Allen?"

Chapter Three

ಏ

Allen Thorne's smile looked more like a sneer as he gripped her shoulders, pressing her roughly against the wall.

"Meru, darling, happy birthday." He tried to kiss her but she turned her head in disgust. His fingers tightened, bruising her bared flesh, and he laughed.

"Whatever is the matter, my love? Aren't you happy to see me?"

Not only was she *not* happy, she was still reeling from the truth she'd instantly "seen". Allen Thorne, the liar, cheater and all around jerk extraordinaire, was apparently more than met the eye. The man she used to swear had a silver tongue actually had one that was long and forked instead.

She glared up into his face, watching scales ripple around features she'd once thought attractive.

"It all makes perfect sense now." She struggled against his grip. "I knew you were a snake."

"*Sauros*, sweetheart, not snake." He shook her lightly to stop her movements. "I heard you could 'see' now."

He tilted his head in calm contemplation. "It's funny, really. I honestly believed it would be your cousin in the end. That's why I was almost relieved when you came in and caught me that night. I was tired of babysitting the bait."

He snorted as she flinched. "Who could blame me for not knowing it was you? Sheridan is so much *more*, isn't she? More attractive, more challenging, more hot-blooded…"

His tongue whipped out and she gagged, thinking about the fact that she'd actually kissed this thing. Thank every power in the universe that was all they'd done.

Several things happened in quick succession. Sheridan, who had quietly approached them during Allen's cruel remarks, pulled Meru out of his surprised grip and behind her as she threatened, "Touch her again and you die."

As soon as the words left her lips, Meru heard an inhuman roar of rage. Allen's body went flying from the hallway out onto the pool table, which crashed beneath him from the force. Damon had hurled him away from her, the look on his face so full of barely leashed fury she shuddered.

Finn appeared beside them and raised his hands. A quick burst of light caused Meru to blink rapidly.

Silence.

She looked around. Everyone in the bar had frozen. Everyone that is, except for a few key players—the five of them, now standing around the moaning Allen and the large group of his cold-blooded friends swarming over from the far end of the bar.

They'd hesitated momentarily at Finn's display and Meru heard some of them whisper *"Fianna"*.

Damon, Finn and Val spread out, surrounding her and Sheridan as the surreal scene unfolded.

Damon took a defensive stance. His shirt tightened until the seams began to fray. His muscles seemed to expand and the skin on his face went taut, his cheekbones becoming sharply defined. His lip curled toward the enemy in a menacing snarl, revealing gleaming, elongated canines.

Meru couldn't contain a gasp of shock at the long claws that erupted, razor sharp and deadly from his splayed fingers.

His transformation seemed to end there and a part of her was relieved. She wasn't sure she was ready to see the man she'd been lusting after go furry all over. As it was, his sheer presence was enough to terrify the enemy.

She felt a flutter in her stomach and knew it wasn't fear. He looked so powerful, so primal, and she was reminded of last night's erotic fantasy. Had the scene in the forest been a premonition? Was he the lover she had begged for in her dreams?

The loud hissing of the nearing *Sauros* pulled her back into the present with a terrifying jolt.

The blond named Val threw his head back and yelled out a battle cry. "*Hawk frithr berserker!*"

Before Meru could blink, a hawk appeared above their heads. The bird was impossibly large, swooping low, screeching in rage. She looked instinctively at the blond's rippling biceps. The tattoo was gone. *Holy Hannah!*

Finn pulled a sword out of thin air, dropping the long, thick blade into Val's waiting hands. The mass of reptiles paused once more, intimidated.

"Cool!" Sheridan's softly uttered words drew Meru's attention. Her cousin, who had been slack-jawed with shock, seemed to have bounced back quickly enough. Unfortunately, so had the bad guys.

"Oh, that is lovely," Finn grunted, acid in his tone as he tossed a *Sauros* over his shoulder. "I place an entire bar full of people in protective suspension, she says nothing. The Viking's theatrics, on the other hand..." He rolled his eyes and focused on the fight.

He kicked another leisure-suited Gila monster easily across the room. It looked like he was going to hit a table full of frozen patrons but he didn't. Right before he would have bowled them over, the forked tongued fighter hit some kind of invisible energy barrier and bounced painfully off it before falling with a thud to the floor.

It seemed to Meru that the Lizards were multiplying. She hadn't thought there were quite so many of them. Damon and the others were clawing, hacking and punching through them like butter, leaving fallen bodies in their wake, but more kept coming. It became clear to her within moments that it was her they were trying to reach, their eyes following her smallest movement.

"Who *are* these guys?" She heard Sheridan whisper to her as she lifted up the leg of her jeans, pulling out a small 9 mm from her ankle holster.

"And why does your ex-boyfriend, who you never told me was such a prick by the way, suddenly look like a refugee from Snake town?"

"Wait, you can see that?"

Val, who'd backed them against the wall to protect them as the others dove into the fray, said almost conversationally over his shoulder, "They've dropped their glamour, little seer. Maintaining it takes an energy they can't really spare right now." He watched with pride in his eyes as the hawk dove, talons first, on the panicked *Dark*.

Damon, upon hearing Sheridan's comment, stopped and turned in disbelief, apparently not remotely concerned that he'd left himself vulnerable.

"You're dating a *Sauros*?"

Though Meru couldn't really blame him for the disgust in his tone, her hackles rose defensively. The terror that had been overwhelming her since this surreal altercation started faded into the background for a moment.

"*Was* dating. As in nearly a year ago," she called over Val's shoulder. "It's not like I knew he was lizard. A two-timing, mean, nasty snake in the grass, sure. But not an *actual* lizard. Damon, look out!"

His clawed hand shot out without turning from her, knocking down the lizard who'd had him in his sights. She sighed in relief, irritation forgotten.

Meru looked away first, noticing that the few *Sauros* not lying still on the beer-soaked floor had disappeared, leaving Thorne alone to his fate. Where had they all gone?

Allen had recovered from his collision with the table and he circled the growling Damon warily. The normally well-groomed, perfectly coifed man wasn't looking so hot now.

Blood poured from deep gouges in his face and side, courtesy of several taunting swipes from Damon.

Allen grimaced humorlessly through the pain. "You should just give her to me now, *Fianna.*" He reasoned. "We are not the only ones after her."

Damon stepped closer to him, snarling dangerously.

Thorne held up his hands. "Be reasonable. You would endanger your warriors over a nothing? For what? The chance to find out for yourself what it feels like to fuck a fat, frigid bitch? Even I wasn't willing to go that far."

Damon raised his massive arm high and leapt forward, his intent clear, but an instant before his dagger-like claws met sneering scales, something happened. He turned in midair, spinning out of the way just as a bullet streamed past his head to pierce the scaly arm Allen had raised in defense.

The *Sauros* let out a grating screech as he slid to the ground. Slipping his hand inside his now ragged shirt, he gave a nasty smile.

"How is your mother, Sheridan? Please, give her my best." Then he simply vanished. No flash, no puff of smoke—just nothing.

Silence descended over the debris-filled room. For long moments, only the heavy breathing of the men broke through the oppressive quiet.

Damon stood with his back to them, his body shuddering, muscles rippling, and Meru instinctively knew he was attempting to reverse his partial transformation. How she knew was anyone's guess. But she didn't question it. He let out a frightening growl as he punched a clawed fist through the wall nearest him. After a moment his shoulders relaxed, his claws retracting as he regained control.

He turned, walking slowly toward the women, anger still a living flame in his eyes as they traveled between Sheridan and the gun clenched tightly in her hand.

She stared him down without apology. "He hurt Meru."

He nodded in understanding. "Next time, a little more warning would be appreciated. I like my hair this length."

It was obvious as he offered a thin-lipped smile that he was trying to put her cousin at ease. She wasn't surprised at all by Sheridan's actions—she had always been a little overprotective. Meru was just glad Damon hadn't been hurt.

His eyes focused on the bruises already forming from Thorne's rough handling of her shoulders. His jaw clenched hard, his hands curling into fists and she knew he was angry that she'd been hurt. Something warmed inside her at the thought.

Finn looked at the carnage around them. "I suppose we're on their radar now." He didn't sound at all unhappy with that turn of events.

It was then that Meru noticed the hawk had disappeared, though the fallen *Sauros* still littered the ground. The bar itself was an unrecognizable heap of broken glass and splintered wood.

Her dazed eyes looked around in shock at the bloody mass of reptilian bodies around them. The frozen revelers were still oblivious, thank heavens. She couldn't imagine what the sight would do to them all. She knew she'd never be able to forget it.

She looked down at her trembling hands, then back at Damon's still form. His narrowed eyes looked deeply into hers before he opened his arms. She hesitated only a moment. Though she'd just met him, it was the most natural thing in the world to step forward and allow herself to be wrapped in his protective embrace.

Turning her head, she pressed her cheek against his pounding heart in time to see Sheridan run a surprisingly shaky hand over her face. Her cousin walked in slow, measured steps to where Finn stood eyeing the wreckage. His unusual eyes warmed with compassion as he too opened his arms to offer comfort.

Lifting the Veil

Sheridan promptly smacked his hands away, causing him to step back in surprise. "Thanks all the same, Mr. Freeze, but I don't need a hug. I need help."

Finn tensed with what Meru thought for a moment might be an expression of hurt. It was gone so quickly she might have imagined it and he leaned his back against the nearest wall, raising his eyebrow in cool disdain. "That, my dear Ms. Kelly, is woefully apparent."

She ignored him and walked over to the table where their friends sat statuelike. Pointing to her partner, she demanded, "Release Kyle."

When he didn't seem inclined to do so, Sheridan clenched her fists and took a threatening step forward. "Didn't you hear that—that reptile? He's going after my mother!"

"Aunt Lily!" Meru pulled herself out of Damon's arms as the three men straightened, instantly alert.

Val nodded, looking at the fallen bodies in concern. "It was an obvious threat. I've never seen so many *Sauros* in one place. Not for centuries. And we know at least one of them was in possession of an Archon transport device."

At Meru's curious look, he explained, "*Sauros* can't flash away like Finn and his people can—and they aren't smart enough to make one of those things on their own. Myrddin wasn't mistaken, this does not bode well."

Damon turned on Meru, frustration and suspicion warring in his gaze. "What do they want with you? Who *are* you?"

"How would I know? Allen said something about—" She shrugged in confusion, completely at a loss. She was nobody special. Allen was right about that, if nothing else.

Damon seemed to read her thoughts as clearly as if she'd spoken aloud and pain and regret filled his eyes. He reached to take her back into his arms, only to be stopped by a familiar voice.

"She, Damon Arkadios, is your assignment. Direct descendent of the High Priestess Áine. The only one who can save us from what is coming."

"Talk about a dramatic entrance," Finn said. "Now *that's* a pretty boy." Val nodded in sober agreement.

"Raj?" Meru asked in disbelief.

Her friend stood before her, still as perfectly beautiful as ever. Almond-shaped eyes a striking emerald green against the dark gold of his skin. Full lips and a strong, angular jaw framed by a straight fall of jet-black hair that he always wore in a thick plait down the middle of his back. He was tall and broad-shouldered, though his movements held the lithe grace of a dancer. He'd always seemed a little otherworldly. Now she knew why. Meru sighed, overwhelmed by the night's revelations.

He had appeared in the same way that Allen had disappeared moments before, and she could see clearly that he too was more than human. Stunning gold-and-ruby-colored energy whirled around him and Meru saw in her mind's eye the image of a powerful dragon.

Raj was a shifter too?

"You know him?" Damon asked, jealousy in his tone. Raj just smiled and stepped forward to take her hand.

He looked toward the pacing Sheridan. "I am to take you to Miss Lily as soon as we get this mess cleaned up." His eyes grew sad. "She will need you both this night. She has lost much to the *Dark* ones."

Sheridan stepped closer. "Then she's alive." Meru saw the shudder that passed through her cousin at the news. "Tell us exactly what's happened. Is she hurt?"

"She is fine. Her shop did not fare as well." He looked at Meru in apology. "It's gone. All of it. The first responders managed to contain the blaze but...The Willow's Knot is gone."

Meru stumbled back, held up only by a silent Damon, his hands gripping her shoulders in wordless comfort. His presence soothed her but she honestly wasn't sure how much more she could take.

Poor Aunt Lily! That shop was her whole world. Their whole world. The only true home they'd ever known. And it was gone? Who would do something so horrible?

Allen's scaly visage appeared in her mind's eye.

This is my fault.

But why? And what on earth had Raj been talking about before? Did Professor White know his friend was a dragon shifter?

Stupid question, Meru. He had given her the book after all.

Sheridan had been very still and quiet. Once he'd finished speaking, she'd watched as Raj and Finn had used their abilities to clean and restore the bar and remove the corpses. When Raj announced it was time to leave, she laid her hand resolutely on Kyle's shoulder.

"Unfreeze my partner. Now."

"Oh, for Danu's sake—" Finn's angry outburst surprised them all. "We don't have time for this!"

"Finn." A look passed between the two men and Damon raised his brow. Raj stepped forward to get Finn's attention. "It's all right. Myrddin needs Kyle's help as well. He specifically requested I bring him."

Finn gritted his teeth as Sheridan smiled in triumph.

He stormed up to her and placed his hand on Kyle's other shoulder. "Put your arms around me," he ordered grumpily. When she leaned away from him instead, he glared. "I'm taking you *and your partner* to see your mother, you ungrateful wench."

Sheridan sighed but stepped forward to wrap her arms around Finn's neck.

He immediately used his free arm to pull her closer, his eyes closing at the sensation. "See?" He silkily intoned. "That wasn't so hard, was it?"

"Not hard at all." She made a face at him and his smile took on a wicked gleam.

"Give me time, Sher. Give me time." Then, in a flash, they were gone.

Meru turned to see Val covering his mouth on a cough that sounded suspiciously like laughter. Raj reached out his arm to take her to her family and Damon snarled, causing Meru to jump in reaction. But he made no move to stop them.

She looked sideways at Raj, demanding, "Is anybody planning on explaining this to me anytime soon?"

Raj nodded. "Myrddin will answer all your questions, Meru."

"Who the heck is Myrddin?"

Her words echoed after they, too, popped out of sight.

Damon looked around the bar, his movements calm as he stood guard over the still frozen patrons and waited for Finn to pop back in and pick them up, but his mind was in turmoil. He was concerned about what he'd seen and sensed tonight, his own feeling of foreboding joining Val's.

He was less than pleased that Myrddin had given them so little to go on, putting a lot of humans in potential danger in the process. He was half mad, however, at the already untenable situation with his newly discovered charge.

Meru was his responsibility. The heretofore unknown priestess. A more dangerous situation he could not fathom. Look at what had happened tonight. He'd been so lost in his lust for her, so blinded to the danger around them, that she had nearly been taken. How could he protect her from the *Dark* and their machinations? He wasn't even sure if he could protect her from his own beast's desires.

He didn't have any answers and his control was tenuous at best. His vision blurred and he felt the wolf stir as he recalled her in Raj's arms. He would have to find a way to work this out. This new possessive fire pulsing through his veins would have to be dealt with. One way or another.

Finn returned and worked his Magick on the silent crowd, ensuring that they would be free after their departure and recall only that they had had too good a time. As he watched, Damon made a decision. He would protect her from the *Dark and* from the Lycan half of him, whatever the cost.

What he wouldn't do, though the civilized part of him knew it would be the right thing, was stay away from her. He and his devil agreed on one thing. They both wanted Meru. Were determined to have her. And frankly, he was sick and tired of every Tom, Dick and Dragon taking her away from him.

Chapter Four

As soon as Meru realized Damon didn't have the same abilities as Raj, she demanded he return for him. Another wave of *Sauros* could be swarming through the bar doors that instant, outnumbering the two men left to fend for themselves.

She was more than a little frantic when Raj made her guzzle down some sort of herbal concoction. She felt its effects immediately. Her thoughts seemed crystal clear and she calmly accepted Raj's assurances that Finn would bring the others shortly. That's when she realized where she was.

The professor's library.

It had always been her favorite spot in the old man's home. Several long, comfortable leather couches framed a stately marble fireplace. The mantle was cluttered with interesting artifacts, as well as most of the knickknacks he had purchased from The Knot.

Books of every shape and size lined the walls and the wood floors were decorated with the loveliest Moroccan throw rugs. It was a cozy, safe-feeling room.

And it was occupied. They'd walked in from the foyer to find Aunt Lily and a broad-shouldered stranger sharing a rather torrid embrace.

Sheridan, for some odd reason, popped in with Finn and a still motionless Kyle several moments *after* Meru arrived. Already a tad flustered, she was quite a bit worse off when she caught a glimpse of her mother's surprising lip-lock. No doubt, Meru serenely decided, because she refused the drink Raj had offered her.

Though Lily looked more fragile than usual, she still laughed off both Sheridan's indignant huff and the man's blushing excuse of offering comfort. She inspected Sher and Meru hugging them tightly in relief when she realized they were unharmed.

As soon as she saw those distinctively silver eyes, Meru knew who the tall, clean-shaven man really was. Professor M. White. *Myrddin*. Another name, she recalled as Raj's drink did its job, for Merlin. That would explain the sparkling nimbus, hovering crown-like above his head.

Not even remotely old and doddering anymore, *this* man was mature, but still striking. With salt-and-pepper hair, a dark, exotic, attractively lined face and a finely cut figure, he did not remind her of her dear old friend at all. Except for those unique, twinkling eyes.

Fletcher arrived with a heavily laden tray of fancy-looking *hors d'œuvres*. He seemed to be avoiding her more than usual. Refusing to meet her eyes. She stepped in front of him and grabbed a well designed cracker to nibble on.

"Fletcher?"

He sighed. "Yes, Miss Meru?"

She nibbled quietly for a moment. "Were you aware that you had a tail?"

He shifted the tray in his hands and sighed again. "Yes, Miss Meru."

She nodded soberly, then leaned in a little closer. "Well, I think it's quite dashing."

The slender man jerked his eyes upward as if to confirm her sincerity, near blinding her with the brilliance of his smile. Had he been worried about her reaction?

She had to admit, if she hadn't had that miraculous potion of Raj's, she might have been a bit taken aback by her favorite persnickety sidekick's appearance. She was seriously considering talking that cute dragon shifter into marketing the stuff. It wasn't Fletcher's conservative clothing that had changed. But the rest of him was definitely an interesting surprise.

The professor's Guy Friday, who'd always seemed rather nondescript and average, his face forever puckered in a scowl...had changed. Fletcher was actually quite beautiful, a magical image straight from the pages of her old textbooks. He had slender pointy ears, a long, highly active tail and a slight powder blue tint to his skin that was deepening in hue as she continued to stare. Even his hair and heavily lashed eyes were that same, striking color.

"Lovely." Meru sighed.

His grin widened, gratitude in his gaze as she snuck another cracker from the tray.

She strolled over to where Kyle, having been released by Finn before the Fae had disappeared again, was listening carefully to Sheridan and Raj. They were attempting to fill him in on his missing time. He looked like a confused teddy bear. Shaking his shaggy brown hair out of his eyes and scratching his beard as he usually did when he was thinking hard about case, he listened.

"Are you sure somebody didn't slip me a Mickey?" he asked hopefully. "Or maybe I have malaria. Are there spots on my tongue?" He stuck out his tongue.

It was obvious Kyle was trying to ease the tension he sensed in his friend and partner. There was, however, no doubt of Sheridan's veracity in his eyes. The two had been through too much together, Meru knew, and Kyle, just like her cousin, was nothing if not loyal to a fault.

Meru knew the moment Damon arrived in the house. She sensed him with an excited shiver. *Thank goodness.*

He burst in from the front hall, tension in every line of his frame until his gaze caught hers. Dark, worried eyes took silent inventory, his body only relaxing when he was satisfied she was all right. Finn and Val sauntered in slowly behind him, unconsciously spreading out to take up protective positions around the three women.

Myrddin stood and walked to the fireplace in the center of the room. He turned and looked at Meru. "Where to begin?" he pondered aloud.

"How about where my cousin was attacked and snake men started popping up all over my favorite blues bar?" Sheridan pounced, storming toward him defiantly. "Or I know. How about where you suddenly get thirty years younger and try to take advantage of my vulnerable mother? Better yet," She was on a roll. "How about—"

"Sheridan Margery Kelly! That's quite enough." Meru ducked her head in a respectful reflex. Lily had to be upset if she was pulling out The Voice.

Finn, who had perched on an arm of the couch beside her, snickered. "Margery?" A speaking glance from Damon silenced the Fae.

"I can only imagine how hard this must be for you," Lily began firmly. "You've always denied your heritage, been embarrassed by it *and* by me." Sheridan's braid swung with her vehement denial but Lily hushed her.

"I let it go because I know how difficult it is to be different when you're young. Maybe it was irresponsible of me but I wanted the two of you to grow up happy...and safe." She lifted her hand to her daughter, her other grasping behind her, reaching for Meru, who came quickly to her side.

"Our family *is* different, Sher. It always has been. Those stories I told you as a child? Well, for the most part, they were all true." Sheridan ripped her hand away from her mother and began to pace.

Meru stepped in her path. "Sheridan, let's hear them out."

Her cousin faced her, every inch a warrior.

"How are you so calm?" she demanded forcefully. "Why aren't you freaking out right along with me?"

Meru shrugged, laughing softly. "Well, it could be Raj's tea. Or it could just be the day I've been having."

She took Sheridan's hands, turning her away from their rapt audience.

"All day long I've been seeing what you saw tonight. Those snaky...um...*Sauros* guys. One of them even turned out to be my ex." She felt Damon tense and she shifted uncomfortably.

"For heaven's sake, look around you, Sher. We're in a room full of Shifters and Faeries and Druids."

"Oh my."

Meru looked over at Kyle, who'd slapped his hand apologetically over his mouth with a shrug. Her quelling look hopefully stopped any future *Wizard of Oz* references.

She turned to Val, eyebrows raised. She still didn't completely understand what it was she "saw" when she looked at him. Catching her silent question as to how he fit into this supernatural melting pot, he smiled and waggled his fingers.

"Cursed Viking," he said helpfully.

Meru's eyes grew wide. "Um...okay."

She looked at Sheridan and jerked her thumb toward the blond. "We've even got a cursed Viking." She repeated dutifully. "Who can do really cool tricks with his tattoo."

Sheridan smiled as the others laughed, thankful for a moment without tension.

Meru pulled Sheridan's forehead down to lean against her own. "What will change if we do go nuts about it? It can't hurt to hear them out, can it? Isn't the detective in you just the least bit curious?"

Sheridan nodded, hugging Meru quickly before returning to the sofa beside her mother.

Meru looked over at Damon, reddening at the obvious admiration in his eyes before turning toward Myrddin. Pride shone in the older man's mercurial gaze as he kissed her fingers in his habitually gallant way.

Neither of them saw the restraining hand Val calmly placed on Damon's shoulder. "I just knew you would do well."

"I'll let you in on a little secret, Prof—Myrddin." Meru leaned in conspiratorially. "I'm not really doing all that well."

He nodded, smiling softly in understanding. "You've been through a lot tonight...all of you." His voice rose to include the others. "There is much to tell but we should give Sheridan's justified concerns about your safety top priority."

At his look, Damon stood and gave a succinct recount of the unusual skirmish. "There's something else." Myrddin motioned for him to continue. "There was a familiar scent prior to the attack."

Myrddin appeared to understand his meaning immediately, though he seemed surprised. "Ahh, I see. Theron or Kyros?"

"Both," Damon bit off roughly. "And their scent was all over the *Sauros* as well, which can only mean one thing. Though I can't imagine what would tempt either of them to work together this way."

"Not to mention who," Raj added in his calm, musical voice. "That transport icon can only mean one thing. These *Dark* appear to have friends in high places."

All the men nodded in mute agreement.

"Let's pretend I have no idea what any of you are talking about." Kyle's voice broke into the sudden silence. "Pretend I'm just a puny mortal detective that didn't even get to *see* any nasty lizard action since he was frozen, missing every damn thing." He scratched his beard thoughtfully.

"The quote, unquote 'Bad guys' are after my partner's family. *My* family." He emphasized. "The real question here is why? Why them? Why now? And why do you all seem to think that Meru is their primary target?"

Myrddin's expression grew grave "I don't know."

The men of the *Fianna* made scoffing sounds of disbelief and Meru silently agreed. Sure, he'd been pretending to be a normal old man when she'd known him, but even then there didn't seem to be anything the man didn't know. At least, not that he'd admit out loud.

"I know why you are important to *us*," he looked at Meru. "And I know why the *Dark* would do everything in their power to get their hands on you." His brow furrowed in confusion.

"What I don't know is *how* they found out about you in the first place. And if the *Sauros* calling himself Thorne is to be believed, they've been aware of your family for a while now." It obviously pained him to admit it.

Meru put her hand on his shoulder, her mind reeling. "Why me?"

"You're a daughter of Áine, favored by Danu." Meru turned to eye Finn as he answered quietly, for once lacking his usual irreverence. "And from what I've witnessed tonight, you are also *banfhlaith*, a true seer." He looked to Myrddin, who nodded in confirmation.

"No, I'm not." Meru denied adamantly. "I didn't 'see' anything until I recited that ridiculous spell the Prof—I mean Myrddin gave me."

"That ridiculous spell, as you call it, wouldn't have worked for just anyone, Meru," Myrddin averred firmly. "Only one of true Druid descent, who already had the gift inherent within them, could have harnessed the power of that particular invocation."

"And," he continued when she would have interrupted, "only a *banfhlaith* of Áine's line could successfully hold and read the Book of Veils."

Her shoulders slumped, though she wasn't sure if it was out of relief or disappointment. She hadn't really wanted those scaly psychos chasing her, right? She saw Damon hovering protectively out of the corner of her eye and sighed. She had a feeling she might miss being the focus of that particular predator.

"That clinches it." She looked Myrddin right in the eye. "You have the wrong girl."

When he raised his brow she was forced to admit, "I couldn't read the book, all right? All I saw were blank pages. And now that The Knot has burned down..." she hesitated when her aunt inhaled shakily. "We can't even find out if Sheridan or Aunt Lily were the ones who could see the contents. There's just no way a book that old and fragile could have survived the fire."

Myrddin lifted her chin with a delighted laugh. "You cannot escape Fate so easily, Ms. Tanner. Not only are you underestimating this particular book's gifts of elusion, but yourself as well. I would be willing to wager quite heavily that you, busy day that you've had, haven't actually had a chance to look at the book at all since you woke this morning."

"The book is safe? It's here? But how —"

A loud clearing of the throat drew everyone's attention to the doorway, where Fletcher stood waiting. He looked pointedly at the clock on the wall above the fireplace before announcing, "The rooms are all prepared should our, no doubt *exhausted* guests like to retire."

A properly chastened Myrddin nodded. "Quite right. We can finish this discussion in the morning. Tomorrow will be a busy day for all of us."

Silver eyes began to swirl hypnotically as they focused on Meru. His rich, deep voice was compelling.

"Know that you are on safe ground. This house is utterly protected. Nothing and no one can enter without my leave to do so. Go to your room. Relax. Sleep well and free of worry. I will see all of you in the morning."

Meru attempted to reject his order. She still had so many questions! But she found herself, almost trancelike, joining her aunt and cousin at the bottom of the stairwell in the foyer, where Fletcher was waiting to take them to their rooms.

I don't even have any clothes, she thought vaguely, realizing that everything she owned, which arguably wasn't all that much to begin with, was gone. She would miss her books, her one true weakness, most of all. She'd had piles of everything from linguistic texts to romantic fiction scattered around the smallish loft.

She hugged her aunt and said a soft "good night" before Lily escorted the unusually quiet Sheridan into a room at the far end of the hall. Her family was safe. She watched until the door closed behind them. That was all that truly mattered.

Fletcher stood patiently, holding open a nearby door, a gentle smile of empathy on his face. She grinned. Her unconditional acceptance of his true form had obviously been a turning point in her relationship with the man. She nodded in thanks, kissing his cheek shyly before closing the door behind her.

Her eyes widened as they took in the enchanted forest she'd been escorted into by mistake. The room was like something out of a fairy tale. As her gaze fell on the massive bed that dominated the décor, she chuckled. Okay, an X-rated fairy tale.

Lush forest green carpet, which she immediately slipped out of her evil heels to wiggle her toes in, covered the floor of the enormous room. The dresser and side tables all looked hand-carved, one-of-a-kind works of art done in rustic knotty pine.

And, oh, that bed. It was enormous, with four wooden posts she'd be willing to bet she couldn't get her arms around. The spiraled columns sprung up from the bed like majestic old trees. Draped with a scrumptious silken bedspread in swirling shades of emerald and gold and covered in velvety-looking throw pillows, this bed looked ready for anything. Except a single occupant.

She sighed. That bed was not meant for one person, not meant for sleeping at all.

At the foot of the bed, a package of underwear sat atop a comfy-looking pair of cotton pajamas and Meru nearly did a happy dance. "Thank you, Fletcher!"

Now she could handle anything. So what if her life had just turned into a marathon *Buffy* episode? She could finally get out of this embarrassingly revealing, "never to be worn again because it was going in the trash" dress.

Spying the en suite bath with gratitude, she quickly scooped up her treasure and entered her new favorite room. If she'd had any idea the professor's house had hidden this paradise, she might have moved in months ago.

She shook her head. The professor. She'd never be able to think of him as anything else.

The bathroom was as big as her living room and kitchen combined, the style reminiscent of a Roman bath. Complete with marble countertops, a giant gilded mirror which she studiously avoided and a luxurious tub that could easily fit three of her. No doubt about it, she was in love.

She filled the tub with scalding hot water and the lavender bath salts that she had found conveniently sitting on the rim of the tub. Her favorite kind. Stripping quickly, she eased into the water with a blissful hiss. There was nothing like a steaming bath to soothe away the worries of the day.

Stroking the washcloth carelessly over her body, she turned her mind back in the same direction it had been going without her permission all evening. Toward Damon Arkadios.

She took all the rest of the insanity that was today and placed it on a shelf in her mind labeled, "to overanalyze and go crazy over later", and let her eyes close dreamily. And there he was. Damon. Heavens, he was one yummy wolf.

Lycan, she amended with a wicked grin. Call her crazy, but she was oddly unfazed by the fact that she had her first recorded case of lust for someone who grew claws and fangs on a regular basis. So what if he wasn't quite human? He was more. Her aunt *had* raised her to be open to other cultures after all, she reasoned giddily.

She was more convinced than ever that her dream had been a prophetic one. That Damon was the wolf-man that had pressed her down onto that forest floor, filling her with the unfamiliar desire to be subdued. To be taken.

It wasn't just lust she felt for him. Though she had reached thirty and was still, for lack of a better word, *intact*, she was no fool. You couldn't be completely innocent in this day and age, not unless you lived in a bubble.

She'd been known to watch a racy movie or two and she'd certainly read enough erotica. Oddly, the stories where the shifter falls head over paws for a human woman were always her favorite. She even had her own pocket-sized B.O.B. in her nightstand in case of emergencies, or at least she had before it went up in flames.

But, to date, she hadn't met a man who even remotely tempted her to go beyond the requisite goodnight kiss. Not even Allen. *Especially* not Allen, she thought with a grimace of distaste, shaking off the visual.

She wasn't frigid. She was a very touchy-feely person. Unbelievable as it may have seemed, with her studies and her own lack of interest, the issue had just never come up.

Until Damon. Tonight, even amidst the chaos and insane revelations, every time she looked at him, every time he touched her, she'd just wanted to drag him off into some dark corner and do…well…*everything*.

Wicked images flashed through her mind and she pressed her thighs together to still the rising ache.

I really shouldn't be here.

Damon stood frozen, his gaze riveted on the scene before him as the sentence repeated like a mantra in his head.

He had been outside on the balcony that wrapped around the entire second floor, trying to gather his thoughts, when he'd caught her unique scent on the sadistic breeze. And just like the dog he was, he followed his nose to her room.

The glass door was unlocked. He told himself he would just peek in and see if she needed anything, if she was all right. And then he would leave. His eyes were drawn to the large empty bed just as he heard a soft splash through a partially open door.

He was doomed.

The long mirror above the bathroom counter gave him an unhindered view of paradise, all the lush hills and valleys of his own personal Eden. She was a stunning armful, his Meru — those damp curls, her sensual, slightly mischievous expression and a body that made him pant for more.

His cock hardened and a fierce, painful lust clawed at him at the sight of her bare flesh. His gaze followed the slow stroke of her fingers as they fondled the torc she wore around her neck, fingers he wanted exploring his overheated skin.

Áine's family must have passed the torc down through the generations. He remembered seeing it on the priestess. But he never recalled this feeling of possession and lust. Seeing the symbol of the wolf on Meru, his totem, satisfied him down to his uncivilized bones.

A moment later, he lost his ability to breathe altogether, let alone pant as her hand, which had been absently caressing the wolf's head design, lowered to touch one full, creamy breast.

His mouth began to water with jealous desire as her fingers plucked and fondled one rose-colored nipple. He wanted to be the one to touch, to caress those ripe peaks. He could practically taste her in his mouth, his need was so strong.

Her scent called to him again, taunting him. Beads of sweat formed on his brow as he struggled for control. The things he wanted to do to her, things he shouldn't even dream of, washed over him in staggering waves. Her wet pussy gripping him hard as he filled her again and again. Her moans echoing in his ears as he took her hard from behind. He wanted all of it, all of her.

His eyes were drawn to her other hand, where she was making lazy patterns on the soft curve of her belly. Unaware of her audience, Meru slowly slid her fingers lower, down into the dark triangle of curls below. Every muscle in his body locked tight, knowing no power in this dimension could force his gaze away.

Meru was caught up in the most intense bout of fantasizing she had ever experienced. Seeing Damon so clearly in her mind, she would swear she could touch him, smell him. Could almost feel his blunt fingertips caressing her in place of her own.

She gently teased her swollen clit as she pictured them on that theme park of a bed in her room. Naked bodies entwined as they rode each other hard, their harsh breathing and the slap of skin on skin the only sounds in the room. He took her aching breasts in his mouth, plumping and pushing them together with his large hands as he shifted his head back and forth, raining firm licks and teasing nips between the two.

She rubbed the wet lips of her pussy together, sliding a teasing finger around the opening of her sex, imagining that it was Damon's tongue causing the sexual tingle that flowed through her body. Her knees fell further apart as she felt him there, his dark, delicious scent surrounding her.

A soft moan slipped from her throat as she slid one finger inside the snug entrance of her pussy, gathering the moisture there and spreading it in rhythmic circles around her hardened bud, her palm exerting pressure in just the right spot to start her gasping as she visualized his thrusting weight above her. He would be a forceful lover, she knew. Talented and insatiable. And entirely focused on her body, her pleasure.

Damon was losing his mind on a wave of lust.

He roughly palmed the front of his tightening jeans, massaging the aching length of his cock as it pressed against the denim, desperate for the relief he knew he could only find inside her. His fingers gripped his thick shaft, rubbing the head through the fabric in the same rhythm she set for herself. His breath panted out in harsh gasps.

When she arched into her own hands on a groan, a sweetly carnal expression on her face, he nearly groaned aloud.

Her small, pink tongue slid out to wet her swollen lips and he had a sudden, vivid image of her on her knees before him. He could feel those same lips stretched around him greedily, sucking him deep as her tongue lashed his thrusting cock.

He'd teach her how to take him, how to relax and breathe and swallow him whole. He'd sift his hands through those soft, shining curls at her nape and pump himself to heaven in that sexy little mouth.

Meru was whimpering now, her two slender fingers thrusting and circling, faster and faster, slipping out to caress her clit before sliding in once more, nearly dropping him to his knees as he looked on with desperate longing.

Her head rolled against the marble tub as the sweet lavender fragrance of her need wrapped around him and pulled him inexorably further into the room. He had to fuck her. Had to feel that tight pussy clinging to his cock, soaking him.

Take her. Claim her. Mine, the wolf declared aggressively.

He saw black spots in front of his eyes. He tasted blood. And he froze.

One hand slowly reached up to touch the fangs protruding from his gums. He looked down to see that the hand itself was rippling with the change, the nails already growing thicker and lengthening into the claws they were ready to become.

In the swift, silent way of his kind, he backed like a shadow out of the room. As he reached for the knob of her balcony door, he heard her climax, his name a sultry moan in the still room. Damning himself for what he was, Damon disappeared into the night.

He squatted down against the wall outside, his head in his hands as he focused on his breathing, on calming down. He hadn't had to work as hard at maintaining his composure as he had tonight in...well, in at least a thousand years, he thought disgustedly.

He headed around the corner toward his room on the other side of the house. A giant Viking was standing in his path. Looking into eyes that were a light, glowing amber instead of the usual brown, Damon nodded in greeting.

When Myrddin had recruited the conflicted Norseman so long ago, Damon was sure they were in for rough weather. No one understood more than he the difficulties of two spirits sharing one skin. He couldn't even imagine the complexities involved in two strong-willed, sentient brothers vying for control of the same body. Add the fact that one of the twins was a berserker into the mix, and it made for one pain in the ass of a curse.

If it'd been him, Damon was fairly certain he wouldn't have been able to rest until Freya paid in full for what she'd done.

Val and Hawk, surprisingly, had found some semblance of peace together. Val had once told Damon he was used to it. They had, after all, shared a womb. And apart from his brother's annoying mental commentary, it wasn't much different from that.

"Hey, Hawk. Good work tonight." Hawk shrugged and leaned against the wrought iron railing, a glass of whiskey in his hand.

"It wasn't much of a challenge. Though according to Val, what's coming up should be a bit more...interesting."

Damon rolled his neck and ran his hands through hair. "I don't know, my friend. I think I'd rather just skip this one altogether."

When Hawk looked at him askance, Damon chuckled ruefully.

"Oh, I can handle the *Dark*—it's this damn guard duty that may end up killing me."

"But what a way to go." Hawk's smile was sinful. "That warrior woman sure is a fiery one." He paused. "And the little seer? She's enough to make any man long for a big, juicy bite."

One moment Hawk was speaking calmly, the next he was against the brick of the house, the glass shattered on the ground beside him and Damon's hand at his throat. He lifted one dark blond eyebrow mockingly. "Val said she was yours. I was just wondering if you knew."

Damon glared into those cool amber eyes for a moment before sighing angrily and releasing his friend. He stepped away and looked out into the night.

"It doesn't matter. Nothing can come of it." He recalled the scene in the bathroom and his hands fisted at his sides. "I have no control around her."

Hawk leaned once more against the railing, seemingly unconcerned. "And is that really such a bad thing?"

Now it was Damon's turn to look surprised. "How can you, of all people, say that to me? Would you loose the berserker in you on a helpless woman? A woman you had feelings for?"

His handsome face growing hard at the thought, Hawk shook his head in frustration. "Of course not, that's not how it works. Don't be a fool."

He stood straight abruptly and began to pace. "We are similar, Arkadios, but we are in no way the same. As our leader, I have always trusted and admired your instincts, but in this you're blinded to the truth."

Damon stiffened at the insult but Hawk continued. "If my brother and I had only to deal with the berserker, the spirit of the predator within us, that would be a blessing. I was born with it and I have always understood that, though I am a man, I am also the berserker, the deadly hawk." He touched the tattoo on his arm, now a hawk at rest instead of in mid-flight, then looked intently at Damon. "Just as you are the man...*and* the wolf. There is no difference."

"It's not the same, damn it!" Damon growled. "I was not born Lycan! None of us were born to it. Because of one man's black, rotting heart, we were cursed. Not to protect our people but to tear them apart like the beasts we had become."

Hawk sighed. "So you will punish yourself and her out of guilt and fear of what might happen. You'll sacrifice your happiness on the altar of that guilt but at least you'll have your precious control." He looked off into the distance once more.

Damon wanted to deny it but he couldn't. He waited for his companion to speak again, but after a few awkward moments, Damon turned back toward the direction of his room. Before he disappeared, he heard Hawk's voice.

"The wolf mates for life, you know, just like the hawk. He would never harm his life-mate, would die to protect her."

Damon closed the door on that last word, whispering into the darkness, "But what if it's the mating that could kill her?"

His mother's image swam before his eyes and he dropped to his knees. He prayed to the Tuatha's Danu that he would not, after all this time, become his father's son.

Chapter Five

❧

"To translate for our studio audience," sarcasm laced Sheridan's every word, "egotistical aliens from the 'we're better than you' dimension came to Earth to lord it over us humans. When they decided it was too much trouble, they left, locking the door behind them. This ticked off the bad, even *more* egotistical aliens, who had been hoping to play god vs. slave indefinitely." She leaned back, enjoying her moment.

"Now the alien-gone-good and his band of merry supermen play hero by protecting the weak, vulnerable humans from the various dark lords and their evil minions, who, regardless of the aforementioned locked door, still manage to sneak in and stir it up occasionally."

Meru rolled her eyes. Lily choked on a small piece of grapefruit, unable to stem the tears of laughter that welled in her eyes at her daughter's diatribe. Myrddin gently patted her back, fighting his own grin.

This morning's kitchen meeting with her old friend had been confusing, but utterly amazing. Myrddin had lost her a little as he'd tried to explain the dimensional physics behind the portals and the space in which the Archons lived. Meru secretly thanked Sheridan for the clarification, blunt as it was.

"Sounds like a bad B movie, doesn't it?" Sheridan glared at Myrddin's hand, now caressing her mother's shoulders. "Do you really expect us to believe this nonsense, Professor?"

"While a bit melodramatic and rather insulting, you managed to hit most of the salient facts in your usual straightforward way," Myrddin granted her.

"As to your ability to believe, young Sheridan." He looked meaningfully in her direction. "I think the time for *that* particular smokescreen has long since passed."

Sheridan paled, looking disconcerted, and Meru broke into the uncomfortable silence. "Okay, I think we understand as much as we're going to for the moment. I imagine what we need to know more about is how our family fits in? How does my supposed ability to read an old book make us dangerous to the *Dark*?"

Myrddin, who appeared slightly distracted as he watched Lily munching on a slice of pear, muttered absently, "Well, it no doubt has to do with the prophecy."

"Prophecy?" Three female backs straightened in their chairs, their attention now fixed firmly and with great interest on Myrddin. He smiled his amusement and nodded.

"Yes, the prophecy. But before I tell you about that, I must first tell you about Áine, your ancestor." And in that mystical way he'd always had of weaving a tale, Myrddin began to entrance his audience with the story.

Áine was a female Druid, born into the land of Eire during a golden age. The Druids were everything history proclaimed them to be. They'd been a society of *brehons*, or judges, poets, astronomers and natural magicians of great renown. But they were also much older, much more powerful...much *more*.

The Druids were a society of gifted beings, still of the earth, but genetically superior to the average mortal. They were considered by the Archons to be an evolutionary aberration and appeared as godlings to the humans they healed, protected and defended.

They became the bridge between the two worlds, and friends of the Tuatha Dé Danaan, who shared their personal beliefs and many of their abilities with these unique individuals.

The Druids had many gifts of natural Magick. "True sight", "true knowing", elemental manipulation and longevity. Áine herself was born with all the gifts of her kind, enhanced and blazing within in her. She was truly favored by Danu.

She was the high priestess, the ruler of her kind. Áine insured peace, health and prosperity throughout Eire. Warring factions joined together. The Tuatha, always a rather secretive people, allowed themselves to be seen more frequently than they had at any time before or since. It was truly a wondrous era.

Myrddin had known Áine in those days. They'd talked much about the future and their shared gift of "far sight". Áine's visions about the coming extinction of her people and her world worried her greatly. She desperately sought to find a way to aid humanity after she was gone. But try as she might, her sight was never clear enough, or far enough, to find the answers she craved.

It ate away at her until, finally, she called upon Danu, Goddess of the Waters and True Queen of the Tuatha, to aid her in her quest. And Danu, hearing her plea, agreed.

The True Queen created The Cup of Inspiration. A magickal artifact that, when held by Áine, filled with the waters of knowledge. There was, as there always is, a catch. Áine could only drink from the Cup but once, and then only receive the answer to one question.

Myrddin had found her the next day, weeping inconsolably, the Cup having disappeared and her answer to how she could help her people given.

She told Myrddin what she had learned and asked for his help. As she created The Book of Veils, Myrddin worked on creating the Magick to conceal it.

Áine wrote out the prophecy. She neither slept nor ate, pouring her life force, her powers, everything that she was into the enchanted pages. And Myrddin had, by the time he was done, worked a spell so powerful that no Archon nor any mortal, not even time itself, would be able to find or recall the powerful book. Until the point in time Áine had determined it would be needed.

When it was done, Áine was gone, the book had thoroughly hidden itself and Myrddin had, as he had intended, forgotten all about it. He'd begun to remember only nine months ago, when he'd been drawn to seek out Aíne's line. The book, however, had remained unseen, only revealing itself to him a week before Meru's thirtieth birthday.

"And that is why I am at a loss to explain how the *Dark*, specifically the *Sauros*, knew enough to pay attention to you over a year before the spell wore off." Myrddin finished morosely.

"Why do you say that? About the *Sauros*, I mean?" Myrddin tensed at Sheridan's question, his usually magnetic eyes guarded.

"*Sauros* do not usually travel in groups. In fact, in recent years, their attacks have been so random that I had believed them almost extinct. And in all the time I have known them, which is considerable, they have never, *under any circumstances*, obeyed the orders of any but one Archon. And he hasn't been around for thousands of years."

Meru was about to ask him to elaborate, but Fletcher had come in at that point, to Myrddin's obvious relief, and informed Sheridan about the workout room where Finn and Val had requested she join them for some light sparring.

Her eyes had lit up at the promise of some action. Meru could only be grateful that the men had considered that her warrior cousin might need to let off some steam.

Without the calming presence of Kyle, who'd disappeared this morning, apparently under orders to be on the alert for unusual activity and to "keep the women off the radar", Meru could only hope that those immortal tough guys could survive the afternoon.

Lily, standing and stretching lazily after the two had departed, announced she was going to take advantage of Sheridan's absence by having a long soak in her purportedly giant tub.

Myrddin looked inappropriately interested in Lily and her plan, and being so distracted, answered Meru's question about the location of the book before the thought had fully formed in her head.

"It's in you."

"Huh?"

"The Book of Veils. You are the daughter of Áine that called it forth. It will always appear to you when you say these words."

He recited the phrase Meru would need as he was edging toward the door that Lily had disappeared through. It was obvious his mind was on other things and Meru could memorize anything after hearing it once, so she didn't ask him to repeat himself before he strode swiftly out of her sight.

She didn't even want to think of her aunt and Myrddin in the bath together, so she quickly replaced the visual with herself and Damon in the leading roles. She was just getting into it when Raj had appeared to escort her into the library.

Meru took in the view before her, lust and not a little avarice glistening in her eyes. Her mouth nearly watered, her hands twitching with covetous desire as she entered the library and walked to the table that Fletcher had set up for her. The table filled with, according to Raj, some of the most ancient texts and scrolls in existence.

This was what she'd dreamed of all those years in college. All her life really.

"These texts contain the true accountings behind the myths of the ancient world. They've been collected through the years, kept hidden." Raj caressed a tightly wrapped scroll.

"But why hide the truth?"

"After all the wars and hostility in the name of faith and religion, it just made more sense to allow people to believe what they wanted to. For dragonkind and others like us to fade into the background."

How sad. The world could use a little more magic in her opinion.

She wondered for the umpteenth time where Damon could be. She should be grateful he'd been absent all morning. After all the lust-filled dreams she'd had last night, with him in the starring role, she couldn't imagine she could look at him without blushing and stammering like a teenager. Still, she actually missed his presence. It took all her effort not to ask Raj where he'd gone.

"Myrddin told me you might need these texts for references but that most of the information could be found in that book of yours. Where is it by the way?"

She sat at the table, her hands suddenly clammy and her stomach in knots.

Raj looked at her curiously as she held her palms up, cleared her throat and said, "*Leabhar na cailleacha, tar ar ais chugam!*" Which she quickly translated as Gaelic for "Book of Veils, return to me." Fairly straightforward, she thought.

Her arms crashed down toward the table as the weight of the suddenly appearing book made itself known.

"Wow," she whispered, awestruck. Even Raj was impressed. He sat down beside her as she opened the book, giving her a squeeze of congratulations.

She stared at the still blank pages in horror. Shouldn't the writing be visible now? Why would the book appear for her if she wasn't allowed to read it? Her shoulders almost slumped as she asked no one in particular, "Where is the prophecy?"

Raj's fingers closed her gaping jaw gently as the words began to appear in dark, fresh ink on the previously blank page.

"Holy Hannah." She blinked as she focused on the writing before her. She had been expecting more Ogham script, even the Gaelic of the spell, but apparently it was a multilingual book.

"Magick." Raj said serenely at her confused expression. "Just read, Meru." And so she did.

When my time has long gone
And the gods that once sheltered
And governed the earth have turned away.
When the human race has forgotten Magick,
Forgotten themselves
Complacent in their ignorance...
That is when the danger will strike.
The Lords of the Dark will band together against the fading light,
Determined to take back that which was once theirs
With terror and blood.
The guardians of the gateways will stand powerless,
Stunned by the joining.
The raven's shadow will loom large.
But there is hope.
The Great Mother Danu has shown me from behind the veil
How to save our blessed land from eternal night.

"Didn't Damon say something about them joining forces last night?" She shifted excitedly in her chair. Raj nodded, the tension in his body palpable.

"She truly was powerful, this Áine. Though it is a dark future she saw."

"But she said there was hope." Meru clung to those words, trying to tamp down on her own sense of foreboding, before looking down as the writing continued to appear, as if penned by some invisible hand.

The daughter of my daughters will lead the way,
With the True Sight of her inheritance.
She must find the key
Drink in the knowledge of her progenitors
If this world is to have any chance.
Hunted by all,
Her heart must find its mate 'neath a cursed moon
If she is to be saved.

"Oh, I don't like the sound of that at all," she said nervously. Hunted by all? That sounded a little...well...horrifically terrifying.

"The book has stopped." Raj noted. "Those dashes indicate three more stanzas or sections of the prophecy, but they are left blank."

Indeed, she could see that the writing on the page seemed to be reemphasizing the first section, giving her the feeling that this book had an agenda of its own. It did hold the spirit of her ancestor, if she'd understood Myrddin correctly. Áine obviously wanted her to focus on this first segment.

They sat together for a while, discussing the book, its fascinating properties and the prophecy. They decided the book seemed to indicate she was the "daughter of my daughters", as she was the one given the "inheritance" of the book and *banfhlaith* abilities. That, of course, made her even more nervous about the whole "hunted by all" scenario.

Raj was just leaning in close to point out the fascinating line about her "heart's mate" when the door to the library slammed open loudly, causing the two to jump, startled.

Damon stood in the doorway, muscles tight, eyes narrowed as he homed in on the couple huddling far too closely together behind a mountain of books. He watched Raj tilt his head alertly, one animal instinctively sensing the threat from another. Damon bared his teeth in a semblance of a smile.

He remained where he was. The only reason he hadn't leapt across the room to claw the flesh off the dragon was the truth his heightened gifts had quickly relayed to him. He'd smelled surprise, but he hadn't sensed any guilt or, more importantly, arousal.

A pair of shy blue eyes clashed with his before they slid quickly away. Less easily hidden was the adorable blush that stained Meru's cheeks and...there it was, the strengthening scent of lavender and spice. *For him.*

Raj looked toward Meru in question before rising gracefully and heading toward Damon. "I'll be back later," He told her as he stood in the doorway. "Everyone needs to be apprised of what we've discovered today."

Meru nodded distractedly in acknowledgement, but her eyes were repeatedly drawn to Damon, pupils dilating as she continued to stare. He too couldn't seem to stop staring.

He'd taken Detective Mueller to the station house this morning, unwilling to return until he'd known the man would be safe. He'd been loath to leave Meru's protection to others, even one as powerful as Myrddin, but he knew the women considered Kyle's safety just as important as their own. Along the way, he'd found out some interesting information.

"We grew up together," the bearded man had confided. "Sher and I joined the police academy on the same day, Meru cheering us both on." Kyle looked up at Damon, a warning clear in his eyes. "I don't care what you are. But if you hurt that girl..." Damon jerked his head in acknowledgment.

"Not that I think you stand a chance, mind you. I've personally set her up with some of the best guys I know. She shot them all down for one ridiculous reason after another. Too short, too tall, too intelligent, not intelligent enough. They couldn't even get out of the gate."

Damon was secretly pleased with the information.

They passed a nervous-looking man sitting at the front desk leading into the precinct office. Kyle told Damon in a sotto voice about Howard's obsession with Meru and their one disastrous date that had *her* running for the hills—and Howard buying wedding invitations.

Damon had turned to glare at the little man, unaware his eyes had taken on the luminescence of the change or that a low, threatening growl was emitting from his throat.

Poor Officer Delaney had commenced to sneezing so vociferously that he fell completely out of his chair.

Damon's acute hearing picked up the squat man's mumbling as he fumbled to the bathroom.

"Mother was right. This job is too dangerous." *Achoo!* "She's always right."

Kyle, studiously ignoring the commotion Damon was causing, walked him to his and Sheridan's cubicle, sitting down in front of the computer and swiftly pulling up the information on last night's fire. While he scanned the monitor, he cradled a phone to his ear, listening to his messages.

Damon looked around the bustling station, his mind wandering as he thought of the other things Kyle had told him about Meru. About how she'd returned home so suddenly a year ago. About how sad and lost and disillusioned she'd seemed, and how she'd shredded her Master's thesis and refused to talk about it *or* the man she'd been dating with anyone, even Sheridan.

Already overly protective where Meru was concerned, he wanted to find out what or who had hurt her, although he had a feeling the who could no longer be in doubt. Allen Thorne. *Sauros*. He had underestimated them. From their sporadic appearances through the years, he'd never seen that species of *Dark* demonstrate this level of intelligence.

They'd had no one to guide them for thousands of years, those left behind merely aggressive and violent by nature. Scattered, vicious, but easy to kill.

Yet this one apparently spent months covertly moving among humans. And the rest of them, the way they had worked together last night. Had they always been this way or was this new? He knew they'd been half human initially, followers of a truly sadistic Archon who had no qualms about playing with the humans' genetic code.

He had taken it for granted, along with the rest of the guardians, he had no doubt, that their generations of cloning had eradicated everything but instinct and obedience. They'd all been wrong. He'd been wrong. Thorne was proof enough of that. He'd obviously fooled Meru, and in the process hurt her enough that she'd left behind her dreams...her life, because of it.

To Damon, that was reason enough to rip out the bastard's throat.

He wanted to slay her demons. Wanted to keep her safe and see her smiling at him again, the way she did last night. He grimaced as he realized how attached to her he'd become in so short a time. He hadn't expected this intense a connection, bordering on obsession.

Get a hold of yourself, Arkadios.

Myrddin had forced him once, long ago, to study up on the subject of shifter mates, but his own experiences and memories of Lycan lust had overshadowed the romance and passion that he'd witnessed in other *Were* communities. Yet now, here he was, mooning over a woman, every instinct, every part of his being telling him she was the one.

Kyle hung up the phone, a worried look on his face as he relayed the recent activity to Damon. It seemed the *Dark* were fairly ticked off that Meru and her family had yet to be found and were trying to draw them out the only way they knew how. Violence.

A body, identified as a friend and one of Lily's regular customers, was found propped up on the front porch of her house earlier that day. His corpse had been maimed and mutilated, but there were no marks at all on his face, just a frozen expression of horror.

The police had an All Points Bulletin out on the Kelly family, including Meru Tanner, taking it personally because Detective Kelly was one of their own.

At this point, they still believed the family were innocent victims in this, but one or two voices in the media were already speculating as to whether The Willow's Knot had been in financial trouble, looking to connect a possible monetary motive to last night's fire. With no clear trail to follow, and no believable explanation, how long would it be before everyone was looking at Sheridan and her family as suspects?

The detective looked frazzled, telling Damon that once they realized he was in the office, they'd be looking to him for answers. Damon encouraged him to stick to the story. He was to say that he'd told the women to be incommunicado for a while, lying low until Kyle and the boys in blue had a chance to figure out who was behind the recent threats.

His boss might give him hell, but his fellow officers would believe it. Kyle would have their alibis and the *Fianna* would have time to eliminate the threat before the *Dark* could get their hands on his mate. And when the threat was finally contained, well, Finn and Raj could institute their unique brand of damage control.

Damon had given Fletcher the news of Lily's friend as soon as he'd returned, leaving the man in mid-sentence as he'd sniffed out Meru's and The Shambhalan's whereabouts through the closed library door.

Now here he stood, held frozen and mute by the lust coursing through him.

He wanted to take her gently in his arms and carry her back to that enormous bed of hers.

He wanted to pin her to the floor and slam into her wet cunt like the animal he was, taking her again and again until he was so far inside her she'd never be free.

"Should I go and let you get back to flirting with Dragon Boy?"

Apparently, he also wanted to stick his foot as far inside his mouth as it was possible for an antisocial Lycan to do.

Meru, who until that moment had been eyeing him from across the room as if she wouldn't mind either of those scenarios, flinched as if he'd slapped her. She stood, appearing to want to defend herself. Her mouth opened and closed a few times before she plopped back down huffily, taking those beautiful eyes away from him and placing them firmly back between the pages of the book in front of her.

He felt as if he'd been kicked in the chest, all the wind taken out of his sails. Why didn't she yell at him? He could feel her anger but her silence was the worst form of punishment she could have given him.

His insecurities reared their ugly head. *Did* she, in fact, want him to go? Would she rather spend time with the monkish, intellectual Raj?

The wolf inside licked his chops, more excited than put off by the challenge of her apathetic pretense. Meru was *his* and he knew she wanted him. He could smell it on her whenever he came near. He would prove once and for all who she belonged to. He stood watching her bowed head for a single, decisive moment before walking toward the door.

Meru was trying hard not to look up, so angry and hurt and disappointed that he would be such a, well, *man*, that she felt tears prick her eyes. She'd been looking forward to seeing him all day. Then he had to go and open his mouth.

She was startled when she heard the door shut, the distinctive sound of the lock clicking into place.

Her head popped up, heart starting up a frantic drumbeat against her breast as she watched him…there were no other words for it…stalking her. Just like he had in her dream.

He prowled slowly, a true predator. Fluid, dangerous and deadly. His eyes shimmered dark and intense, watching her every movement, her every breath. What she saw in his fiery expression was enough stop her heart altogether. Hunger. Desire. And something more. Something she was sure he didn't want her to see. Vulnerability.

Damon surprised her by kneeling beside her when he reached her chair. He was so tall that she still had to look up to meet his eyes. Every inch the proud Alpha male, he seemed to demand her surrender even as he offered his.

"I don't flirt." She felt obliged to point out, embarrassingly breathless.

"I know."

"And even if I did, I would never flirt with—"

"I know."

"If I *was* to flirt, it would probably be—"

"With me and only me. I know."

"How do you know?" She was perversely put out that he seemed to take it for granted so quickly. "I mean, I *could* flirt with other people, I just *choose* not to. It isn't like you're the only one I can flirt with." But Damon was implacable.

"No. Only me."

"Sure of yourself, aren't you?" She tried to sound confident and cocky, taking a page out of Sheridan's book.

In reality, his nearness was eroding her ability to think beyond the rather primitive, monosyllabic level of—*You. Me. Floor. Now.* And then he ripped even that away from her.

"I'm sure of this." He speared his hands deep into her loose curls, cupping her head to pull her closer. He drew her to him, slow enough that she had time to say no. As if she would, she thought dazedly, before his head tilted and he leaned in closer, his lips just grazing, teasing her own.

Looking into her eyes, seeing the acceptance there, he groaned hungrily as he took her mouth in a scorching, mind-numbing, life-altering kiss.

He ate at her lips as if he was starved for the taste of her, angling this way and that, desperate to get deeper, to taste more. His tongue demanded entrance and she opened willingly, more than a little frenzied herself as she joined his foray with one of her own.

Her tongue tangled and fought with his, sucking him deep into her mouth, savoring the flavor that was uniquely his. It was exotic and addicting, like dark chocolate and sin. She couldn't get enough, couldn't get close enough.

He'd turned her in her chair to kneel between her legs, pressing his rock hard stomach against the already soaked vee of her thighs. She'd never been so excited. So *wet*. When he ripped his lips away to growl low against her neck, she wondered if he could feel her need through their clothes. She didn't have to wonder for long.

He inhaled deeply, shuddering with the effort to rein in his desire. "Gods, Meru, *your smell.*" He rasped roughly. "I could get drunk on it, on you."

He took one tight nipple into his mouth and suckled and laved it greedily, wetting the cloth of the tank top and bra. He nipped at the tender flesh, causing her to whimper and arch toward him. As his mouth moved to her other breast, she felt his rough, calloused fingers slide up the loose leg of her shorts, lightly skimming over the damp lace of her underwear before moaning against her breast. This was so much better than the fantasy, she thought giddily.

"I have to taste you."

He easily moved her on the chair, her jean shorts flung to the floor behind him before she could blink. She fell against the back of the chair as he gripped her thighs in his large hands, positioning her legs over his shoulders, glancing up at her gasp.

His black eyes had taken on a strange sheen, swirling light in bottomless orbs. She couldn't believe this was happening. She'd never wanted anything so desperately in her life.

"Don't worry." He intoned gutturally, misreading her gasp as one of apprehension. "I'm still in control."

Dipping forward, he inhaled her scent with obvious relish. She flushed, but pushed her hips closer to him, needing more. He pulled the lace to the side to reveal her sodden curls.

"So pretty," he rumbled. "So wet and creamy and *mine*. I have to taste you." He gave her no time to think as he lowered his head and licked a path to her clit, giving it a teasingly light swirl before plunging deep, spearing her core with his oh-so-talented tongue.

Their groans mingled in the quiet room as Damon rooted deeper, licking and sucking and nibbling on her swollen pussy lips before thrusting inside again, gathering more of her cream on his tongue, savoring the taste.

She grabbed his head and thrust against him, mindless. She felt something building within her, something huge and frightening and wonderful. She had no idea it would feel like this.

His tongue, that amazing appendage, was doing something so intimate, so wholly foreign to her that it felt forbidden and sinful. And it was making her crazy. She'd given herself orgasms before but she had a feeling she'd never experienced anything like the one she could feel, hovering, just out of reach.

Her head rolled back on a panting moan as one thick finger thrusting inside her snugly. Her internal muscles tightened around him and he grunted in rough approval before adding another, curling them upward to touch a spot that she hadn't known existed.

He paused for a moment before taking her pulsing clit gently between his teeth and growling, causing her to cry out at the low vibrations that ran through her flesh at the sound. Her breath caught on a sob as he pushed through the wet, swollen tissue, past the untried tightness his thick fingers had found.

She felt a pinch of discomfort at the foreign fullness. A growl of hot possession ripped from his throat and it was enough to throw her over the edge. Before she could drag in a breath to cry out at the sensation, he was there, swallowing her screams with his mouth, the taste of her on his tongue wicked and arousing. She pressed against him, searching out more of the taste, only to hesitate at the feel of the unusually sharp canines against her lips.

Damon tensed, his grip on her tightening. Then she was floating, flying, still trembling with the aftershocks of the most intense orgasm in history. When she landed, Meru was bent over the buttery leather of the couch, ass up, feet dangling in the air.

He held her still with a hand on her back when she tried to wiggle around to face him. He saw her peeking at him through the tangled ringlets over her shoulder. He raised his other hand to stick his two, still wet fingers in his mouth, moaning at the rich, honeyed taste of her. She blushed in amazement, then licked her lips as her eyes honed in once more on his mouth. He swore under his breath, desperate to maintain his control.

He'd already been overwhelmed by the taste and smell and feel of her in his arms. When he'd slid his fingers inside her, feeling the snug channel, the scent of her need, her innocence filling his nostrils, the Lycan half of him roared in ecstatic need. He would be her first. The first to claim her. And the last. If there had been the slightest chance before, Damon knew now that he wouldn't be able to hold back.

"Turn around, Meru." He ordered huskily. When she didn't immediately comply, he pressed his body against hers, thrusting once in helpless need before speaking softly against her neck.

"I'm hanging by a thread here, baby." She shivered as he breathed hotly against her sensitive flesh. "Do you want me inside you, Meru?"

His fingers slid over the curve of her lace-covered bottom. They curled around the fabric to tear the offending barrier away. His hand caressed a soft bare cheek, slipping down and entering her once more and this time there were three fingers pumping into her tight sheath. She groaned as he stroked her, stretching her, readying her for his penetration.

"You're so tight, Meru. So damn tight and hot against my fingers. Is it too much?" She shook her head, near weeping as he thrust faster.

"I hope not. I hope you want more. I hope you can take more because I need to get inside. Need to feel you gripping my cock like a scalding, wet fist while I fuck you."

She felt herself squeeze against his fingers, unable to hold back her passion-filled cry at his wicked words. "*Please*."

"Please what, baby?" His fingers tangled in her soaking curls in a soothing caress before tugging gently in a way that made her press against his hand. She could hardly breathe, she had no control over her body. Barely able to move, let alone touch him. She only knew she needed more.

"Please…fuck me," she whispered. Too turned on to be embarrassed by the words or the needy whimper that escaped along with them.

He moved away from her, her moan of disappointment almost drowning out the rending tear and rapid shuffling behind her before he was pressed fully against her once more, whipping off her shirt and bra until there was nothing between them but hot, naked flesh.

"I will," he assured her in a deep, growling voice that seemed not his own. "Just hang on. And close your eyes." She obeyed him, merely because it seemed like too much work to argue, to keep her eyes open, her head up.

Her body turned to liquid fire as she felt the unbelievably hot, hard proof of his desire brush temptingly over her swollen flesh, sliding easily between her dripping folds. The head of his cock entered her and retreated, teasing her, making her want to scream. Her muscles shook with the force of her need, hips wiggling to try to get closer, to push him deeper.

"*Please*, Damon."

His hands were hot on her hips, the hard probing of his massive cock as he positioned her for his thrust making her tremble with anticipation. He pushed inside slowly, burning her, stretching her impossibly wide. She'd never felt anything like this, this satisfying fullness. Every fiber of her being was focused on the sensation. It was almost too much. But still she wanted more. More of him. She wanted it all.

The short, patient thrust and retreat of his hips was driving her crazy. She knew he was trying to take it easy, to go slowly for her. But she was way too far gone for slow and easy, had been from the moment he entered the room, and she wasn't about to let him get away with it.

She was out of control and she didn't see any reason why he shouldn't join her. Wrapping her flailing ankles around his thighs, she pushed back forcefully, impaling herself fully on his cock.

Her body arched at the unbelievable sensation. She bit her hand around the scream she was afraid would alert the entire house, feeling him go unnaturally still. She couldn't believe she had taken all of him. Her imagination hadn't done justice to how long and thick – *how much* there actually was of him.

She could feel the sharp prick of his emerging claws against her flesh. Instead of fear, an answering flood of wetness trickled down around the hardened ridge of his arousal and onto her thighs, soaking his length as he pulsed inside her.

He leaned down to lick her ear. "Bad girl. Do you know what happens to bad girls, Meru?"

Gravelly and coarse, his warning voice was the only hint he gave before nearly pulling out of her, a sharp, stinging slap to one pale cheek causing her eyes to open wide in shock.

Was he...*spanking* her? His large palm came down once more on the other side, her helpless position giving her no leverage to escape the punishment. But she didn't want to. Her body shook under the hot lash of sensation. Every part of her on fire for more. For him.

"Such a pretty ass. Lush and pink. So tempting."

All she could do was gasp for breath as she felt the curves of her ass tingle and warm with each successive whack, the heat spreading to her core, causing her inner muscles to spasm instinctively on the head of his cock. He groaned and clenched her hips once more, punishment forgotten as he plunged hard and deep. Straight to her womb.

"*Yes.* Oh, yes." Meru's entire body bowed at the sensation. He began to drive into her, filling her completely with every delicious thrust. She was taken.

One hand left her hip to pinch a nipple between the rough, fleshy pads of his fingertips. Meru knew he was trying to keep from scratching her, but he seemed unable to resist the chance to touch.

Through the loud sound of her harsh breathing filling her ears, she could hear him behind her.

"Oh fuck, Meru, so good, so *wet*." His hips jerked powerfully against her and she could feel his balls slapping against her with every stroke.

"*Mine.*" He groaned wildly. He pulled her legs up and out behind her, sinking even deeper inside her, pressing against that wonderful spot again with every thrust. Without warning, Meru felt herself coming on a blinding wave of pleasure so intense she nearly blacked out.

He felt her pussy spasm around his swollen cock, the bruising grip destroying his control. Damon thrust once, twice more before emitting a deafening roar, erupting long and hot and hard inside her.

As he tried to catch his breath, he realized that his mouth was open against her shoulder, fangs extended. He closed lips around the offensive daggers, kissing her gently before laying his head heavily on her back. He was angry with himself for losing control at all. At least he hadn't hurt her.

He could feel her heartbeat race against his cheek, her scent and his mingling in the air around them. Damon felt himself hardening inside her once more, and knew he couldn't risk his sanity or her safety by taking her again so soon.

Though every cell in his body protested his decision, he dragged his cock slowly out of her clinging sex until he was standing behind her once more. He was mesmerized by the evidence of his mark on her thighs and had to fight the urge to howl.

She was draped across the sofa as he pulled on his jeans. He felt his brow crease, worry replacing lust as he noticed her shaking shoulders.

"Meru?" he called quietly in concern. Her shoulders shook harder.

Was she crying? Had he hurt her? "Baby, talk to me, please." He lifted her from her position and turned her in his arms to find her…laughing. Laughing?

Before he could take offense, she wrapped her arms and legs around him, squeezing him tightly, a brilliant smile on her face. He must have looked confused, because she kissed his cheek, still chuckling softly as she said, "I had no idea. If I'd known *that* was what it was like, I don't think I'd have waited quite so long."

She slid down his giant frame, reaching to pick up her clothing before he spun her back around, pulling her tightly against him. "Meru." She looked up into his eyes, her own widening at the expression she found there. At the feel of his hardening cock pressing once more against her.

"You waited for *me*, Meru Tanner. That," he indicated the couch with a wave of his hand "only happens with me."

Before she could respond one way or another to his high-handed pronouncement, a knock sounded on the locked library door. Blushing furiously, she threw her clothes on swiftly, stuffing her torn underwear in the pocket of her jeans shorts with a mortified huff.

Looking toward Damon, she realized he was still standing there in nothing but his jeans. "Where is your shirt?" she whispered, panicked. He held up the tattered remains of his black t-shirt, eyebrows raised in apology. Her jaw dropped, scandalized, before another, slightly more irritated knock echoed through the quiet room.

He shrugged, walking over to open the door, letting a waiting Fletcher into the room. The blue man looked down his nose at Damon, quite a feat since he was nearly a foot taller, his expression gentling as he turned toward the beet red Meru.

"Everyone has gathered in the dining room for lunch." He looked at both of their blank expressions for a moment before sighing in his overly patient, utterly put-upon way.

"The dining room, should you be wondering, is right next door."

Damon and Meru glanced at Fletcher, then each other, before Meru squeaked and covered her face with her hands in realization. Damon, suddenly recalling his less than quiet climax, actually felt his face heating in chagrin.

He took a step toward Meru, noticed Fletcher hovering protectively and stopped. Excusing himself to find another shirt to put on before joining the others, he sped up the stairs.

He wasn't running away, he told himself as he strode single-mindedly toward his room. At least not from her. He was running from the triumphant, primitive surge he could feel at the knowledge that she was his. And now...everyone knew.

Chapter Six
ಸಂ

She was just starting to relax, positive she could finish eating without making eye contact with the others at the table. She tried to focus on getting back to the library to study the book…and ruminate over the most amazing experience of her life, when she felt a tingling at her nape.

Damon ambled in, nodding at the others in silent greeting before grabbing a plate and sitting down across from her in silence. He seemed just as determined as she was to avoid conversation.

She felt flushed as she popped a cherry tomato into her mouth. Flashes of what they'd done ran through her head, warming her body from head to toe.

Trying to shift unobtrusively in her seat, spearing a leaf of lettuce, determined to ignore her arousal, she caught his gaze. He looked at her from beneath long dark lashes, his stare heated as if he'd picked up on her thoughts.

Her eyes were drawn to his sharp white teeth, sans fangs, as he bit into a tender piece of chicken. She licked her lips. His hands clenched on his fork.

She knew that with his enhanced senses, he could smell her need. The knowledge, far from making her nervous, increased her arousal. Her legs shifted beneath the long table and his fork clattered to the plate, a nearly inaudible growl rumbling from his chest.

She was fairly certain he was going to leap over the table and take her, audience be damned, and that she'd really, really like it, when they were rudely reminded of their audience.

"So, Professor, I didn't know you had pets." Sheridan's loud voice traveled the length of the table, causing Meru's head to jerk in her direction.

Myrddin looked over at her cousin in confusion. "I don't have pets." Sheridan innocently batted her hazel eyes and Meru almost shivered in trepidation.

"Really? Are you sure? I could have sworn I heard an animal howling, almost as if it were in pain, just before we sat down to lunch."

Chaos ensued.

Val choked on his mouthful of food, Finn patting his back vigorously as he smiled at Sheridan with what Meru could only call admiration.

Raj had nearly fallen out of the chair he'd been leaning on, obviously startled and not a little embarrassed at the lack of his usual grace.

Lily's lips lifted, though she was being unusually quiet, sitting closely beside Myrddin as if for comfort.

Meru couldn't seem to blink or close her mouth, utterly embarrassed. Poor Damon seemed worse off, however. He sat frozen, his gorgeous olive skin definitely taking on a pinkish hue.

She was used to Sheridan's lack of filter but he wasn't. Meru began to wonder if a woman had ever teased him, if he'd ever just had fun, ever played.

It was Fletcher who saved the day. Standing in the doorway, his throat clearing more effective than a gong, he looked at the gathering and announced, "I must apologize if I disturbed you with my howling, Miss Sheridan, I was using my free time to...practice."

Every face around the table was riveted to his in shock. Meru noted Myrddin, however, hiding a smile behind his napkin. Sheridan looked suspicious and rather put out.

"*You* were howling? What were you practicing exactly that caused you to make such a god-awful racket?"

Damon flinched as Fletcher looked toward Myrddin, his brow raised. "If I may, sir?" Myrddin nodded, silver eyes sparkling merrily.

Fletcher looked Sheridan in the eye as he removed his jacket. "I'm Changeling." He stated formally. "I have certain abilities, defensive skills inherent to my species. I was practicing this."

His blue form shimmered before his captive audience. With each heartbeat, he became a different animal. Tiger, turtle, owl. Until finally, he shimmered into a giant, powder blue wolf and released a very loud and fairly impressive howl.

No one moved or made a sound as he shimmered back to his original, albeit still interesting form, putting on his jacket with stiff movements. Meru reached for his hand, gratitude and awe in her expression.

"You're amazing. That was incredible."

Fletcher's cheeks turned a dark, enchanting indigo as he squeezed her fingers. "I knew *you* would think so, Miss Meru. Thank you."

Val looked back and forth between Damon and Finn. "Did either of you know he could do that?" Both men shook their heads negatively, looking impressed.

"Now." Fletcher said firmly, stepping back from Meru's hold to stand formally at the door once more. "I will be serving coffee while Mr. Raj and Miss Meru tell you what they discovered today."

How he knew that, Meru wasn't quite sure, but she was so grateful to him for deflecting attention away from her wild, if rather recent sex life, that she would have forgiven him anything.

For the next hour or so, the group shared their findings. Meru and Raj told them about the accuracy of Áine's vision and what they had deduced from what little of the prophecy had been revealed.

Damon told them what Kyle had discovered, after a nod from Myrddin, who'd already told Lily about the death of her friend.

Meru and Sheridan comforted her as she told the rest of the worried-looking table that she had contacted her closest customers, friends and the members of her circle, telling them only that there was danger.

Meru knew that no one would question Lily. Those who knew her also knew that her feelings were rarely, if ever, wrong. So she wasn't surprised when Lily mentioned that most were currently on their way out of town.

They sat back down and she watched Myrddin look lovingly into Lily's watery green eyes. "I am sorrier than you can know for how much you have lost in so short a time."

Meru thought again of her aunt's livelihood, her shop. Lost in a single night. And now this. A man Lily had personally taught and guided, a man who had joined them for family dinners countless times, murdered senselessly.

Lily looked around the table, eyeing each of the men intently before turning her gaze back to their host. "My family has believed for generations that one day we would be called to do something important. The Willow's Knot kept us fed and clothed for years but it was just a place. Places can be rebuilt. As for Peter," she took a bracing breath.

"I will honor Peter as he would want me to. But I cannot help but be grateful that my girls and I are still alive. Thanks to all of you. And they are finally on their destined path. How can I ask for more than that?"

Lily and Myrddin stared at each other, some silent understanding passing between them. The charged moment was broken by the scraping of Sheridan's chair as she stood once more.

Looking agitated, she walked the length of the room before turning back to face the table. "We can't just stay in the

Professor's house forever, nice as it is. We have to find a way to stop these *Dark*, right?"

Meru knew it must be driving her cousin crazy already, being stuck in here. She always wanted to be in the thick of the action, never sitting still for a moment.

"She must find the key and drink in the knowledge of her progenitors if this world is to have any chance." Raj put in quietly. "The only way to stop this is to figure out what the "key" is that Áine was referring to in the first part of the prophecy. I don't think the rest of it will appear until we do."

"Great." Sheridan huffed.

Meru tilted her head in thought, unaware of Damon's heated gaze as her racing mind hit upon the answer. "Drink in the knowledge of her..." she whispered to herself, before leaping up and rushing over toward Myrddin's chair, nearly skipping with excitement.

"Prof—*damn it*—Myrddin!" She stammered.

"It's the Cup. The Cup Danu made for Áine. I'm supposed to find and drink from the Cup!" She quickly repeated the story Myrddin had told them this morning to the others, nearly breathless with her find.

Finn looked disturbed and rather awestruck. "Tuatha lore is very clear and emphatic on Danu's feelings about the enchanted objects. When we first arrived, she gave four divine gifts to my people for their protection and prosperity."

"Oh, I read about this," Meru jumped in. "The Stone of Fal, the Sword of Light, the Spear of Lugh and the Dagda's Cauldron, right?"

Finn looked at her and rolled his eyes. "And isn't *that* horribly insulting? Most people think the Fae are two inches tall with wings, yet they seem to remember those dangerous artifacts with amazing clarity." He nodded. "Yes. The stone, sword, cauldron and spear were all gifts from The True Queen to guide and protect us. But they ended up doing more harm than good."

"How so?" Sheridan jumped in, intrigued in spite of herself.

"It's complicated."

Meru laughed and looked pointedly at Damon. "You men always say that when you don't want to explain yourselves."

"Anyway," Finn continued in an irritated tone. "Our texts say after it became apparent that the objects were more of a danger than a blessing, Danu vowed to create no more, so as to help us all avoid temptation. I admit I was not as inclined as some of the other Fae to wander outside our realm in those days, so I didn't know Áine well. But still I find it difficult to believe that Danu created this Cup of Inspiration at all, let alone for a being not of the Tuatha race."

"Wow. Don't look now, Finn the Fairy, but your arrogance is showing." Sheridan and Finn shared a speaking glare before Val decided to join the conversation.

"Why didn't she just destroy all the objects, wouldn't that have solved the problem?"

Finn shrugged and looked away from Sheridan, saying, "It's said that once enchanted objects are created, they cannot be destroyed. Only hidden."

"Or lost." Meru said thoughtfully, recalling what Myrddin said about the Cup having disappeared after Áine drank from it.

"It stands to reason that if I have enough of Áine in me to call and read The Book of Veils, then I can also drink from the Cup. The prophecy even says as much." She bit her lip in puzzlement. "All we have to do now is find it."

"No, dear Meru, all *you* have to do is find it." Myrddin said gently. "According to Áine's prophecy, you alone must find the key. As much as I wish I could help you, I believe you are the only one who can." He turned from her pale expression with a sigh.

"Finn. Val." Damon's commanding tone had the two men straighten in their chairs, looking toward him, instantly alert.

"We should go back to Ms. Kelly's house, poke around the shop, see if there is anything there the police might have missed. Any clue as to who might be pulling the strings." The two men nodded and rose from their seats without hesitation. He looked at Raj.

"I need you to go keep a discreet eye on our friend Detective Mueller." Sheridan froze at the mention of her partner. "He won't like it but I believe they'll be watching him closely." Raj nodded, disappearing in an instant from where he sat before Sheridan had the chance to ask to join him.

Damon caught Meru's eye. Her pulse sped up, throat going dry, his gaze like a brand on her skin. And then he was gone. Finn put his hands on Val and Damon's shoulders and the three flashed away just moments after Raj, leaving the girls and Myrddin alone at the table. His silver eyes held apology when he also stood as if to leave.

"I have to go for a short time as well." He sighed. "It seems the council has somehow gotten news of the unusual *Dark* activity and they require an update." He didn't look too happy about it.

"Luckily, this house is protected from their prying eyes, so they have the same lack of knowledge of your whereabouts as our enemies." Lily looked up at him with a worried expression but he just grinned and winked mischievously.

"Thank you for your concern, my love, but I have been running circles around those stuffy council members for eons. I'll be fine. As will you. Fletcher will get you anything you need and you'll be perfectly safe here until we return." And with that, he vanished as well.

"Damn, I wish I could do that." Sheridan muttered grumpily. All the women nodded in agreement.

Meru stood and began edging toward the door. "Well, I better get back to work. Fate of the world and all."

Hazel and green eyes narrowed in determination before they pounced, dragging a helpless Meru along behind them.

And that was how, with a little help from Fletcher, the traitor, she ended up sitting on the balcony outside her aunt's harem themed room, glass of wine in hand, Spanish Inquisition surrounding her in the form of pestering relatives.

"Spill it, Curly Locks." Sheridan drawled in her best "detective in the interrogation room" voice.

"I don't care what he said, that wasn't Fletcher making all that noise. It came from the library. Plus I saw both your guilty faces when you came into the dining room."

As she spoke, Meru took a sip of merlot in preparation, knowing she wouldn't be able to avoid them, before whispering guiltily, "It wasn't Fletcher."

Aunt Lily smiled as Sheridan shook her head in mock disappointment. "Thirty years of restraint down the tubes in less than twenty-four hours." She sighed.

"Cops, fireman, cowboys. Navy Seals for crying out loud. All set up by yours truly. All rejected heartlessly by you. They weren't macho enough for you? Oh no, not you." She threw her hands in the air as Lily chuckled at her daughter's antics.

"*You* were waiting to give yourself to a man with a few thousand years under his belt." Meru gasped as Sheridan nodded and said in a humorous aside. "You learn a lot when you hang out with 'Brad' in the workout room…A LOT." She continued as if she hadn't been interrupted.

"You were waiting for a man who is complex and complicated, a man with a tortured soul, a man who goes doggie when he loses control. A freakin' Wolverine wannabe."

Meru snorted, choking on the wine she was sipping in surprise, trying to catch her breath when she heard Lily say calmly, "Wolverine isn't a werewolf, Sheridan, he has superhuman healing abilities and some kind of strange metal attached to his bones."

The two girls looked at the older woman in consternation before she shrugged innocently. "What? I'm a fan."

Meru shook her head and placed her wine on the small table Fletcher had been kind enough to set out for them.

"Damon is a Lycan, not a werewolf, and no, I don't know what the difference is, but according to him, it's there." She looked out at the large trees that surrounded the house and smiled.

"As for as the waiting, Mom was right." She looked over at Lily and the rose-colored energy beside her, remembering their earlier conversation at the shop about finding the right one. Her aunt grew a little misty eyed, and even Sheridan softened, leaning over to give Meru a hug.

"All right," she grumped. "But if you fall in love and get married, just know that Auntie Sheridan is not going to get stuck at home babysitting the puppies."

They laughed as Sheridan continued to joke about her allergy to wolf fur until they were all leaning back, out of breath, but thoroughly relaxed.

"Why didn't you tell us about Allen?" Meru heard Lily's hurt voice breaking into the quiet. She closed her eyes, unwilling to look at the two women who meant so much to her.

"I was ashamed. Oddly, now that I know what he is, it makes me feel a little bit better. But back then, I thought, well, that maybe it was my fault. I should have known better."

"What did he do to you?" Her cousin's voice had that quiet, dangerous tone it got when she was feeling protective. Meru shrugged.

"Nothing too terrible. He couldn't have been more attentive at first, but after about a month, he started to change." She shifted uncomfortably in her seat.

"He started criticizing my weight, my looks. Just subtle digs. He got angry at the drop of a hat. I thought he was just— I was so busy with my classes...my thesis." They nodded at her to continue.

"And then one night, I went back to my office to grade some papers and there they were, going at it like wild monkeys on my desk."

"Who?" Sheridan growled.

"Allen and Dr. Lissa Poitier, my mentor and one of the head examiners I was scheduled to defend my thesis to the following week."

Meru heard them gasp and nodded at their disbelief. "The worst part about it was, between the heavy breathing, they were laughing about my theories, mocking me as they were both betraying my trust."

She felt herself enveloped in the loving embrace of her family, relieved at last to have told them. She'd never kept secrets from either of them before. She hadn't doubted they would react like this. She'd only doubted herself. But never again.

"What a snake." She heard Sheridan mutter. "I wish I'd aimed better."

"*Sauros*, dear." Lily corrected serenely. "And I wish you'd aimed better too."

Meru emitted a watery laugh as they released her, shaking off the past and reaching once more for her wine.

Deciding to change the subject, she peeped at her aunt over her long-stemmed glass and batted her eyes. "Speaking of magic and romance, you seem rather chummy with Mr. Wizard of late."

It was Lily's turn to blush as Sheridan covered her ears and began to hum. "TMI—too much information. My mother is not sleeping with the Professor. She doesn't even know what sex is, what it looks like, how to spell it..."

Meru laughed loudly. "Give me a break. What about all those stories we grew up with about bull riders, barrel racers, bronc busters. Need I say more?"

Sheridan glared at her. "They were stories, Meru, as in, not in my face making goo-goo eyes at each other. Besides, he's an Archon! An alien! Who knows if they even have the right equipment?" Meru nodded soberly, desperately trying not to laugh, while Lily rolled her eyes.

"There weren't *that* many stories, girls. I wasn't celibate but I'm not exactly the Wild West Mata Hari either."

She looked between the two of them before a secretive grin stole across her lovely face. "And for your information, there is absolutely nothing wrong with that man's equipment." Sheridan gulped her wine down greedily.

"I was always fascinated by him, even when he was pretending to be the old professor. And now, well, let's just say that if he ever wore a cowboy hat, I might actually get down on my knees and propose to him myself."

Two gasps filled the air as the girls realized what Lily was leaving unsaid. This woman who vowed to never fall in love with or marry another...who never even joked about it...had just admitted the serious nature of her feelings.

"Wow." Sheridan took another giant gulp of her wine. "Just wow. Both of you? Just like that? Wow." She poured herself another glass.

Meru saw her smile sadly and she was a little stunned. Sheridan had never been without male companionship. At least, not unless she chose to be. She'd always maintained that her freedom was more important, that no man would ever understand or be able to accept her commitment to her career. But something in her cousin's eyes seemed to be telling a different story. There was a longing there that she'd hidden from all of them.

"Before we can focus on my pathetic lack of a love life or my bleak, new existence as a helpless couch potato—" Her melancholy expression morphed into a playful grin. "Tell us, oh wild Meru, what on earth did you do to Tall, Dark and Furry to make him howl?"

* * * * *

"Free at last." Meru sighed softly as she lay across her bed. She *was* grateful for some alone time. There was quite a bit to think about. She loved her family but they hadn't left her alone all day. She really needed to get up and look at the book but that would mean leaving the sanctuary of her room. *Unless.*

"*Leabhar na cailleacha, tar ar ais chugam?*" She uttered the chant hopefully.

"Ooomph!" The book really needed to work on its aim, she thought huffily, picking it up from where it had landed on her stomach and placing it beside her on the bed.

She rose quickly and rushed through a shower, putting on the light, button-up cotton top of her pajamas, before plopping down on her stomach across the giant bed to read.

Opening the beautiful binding once more, she turned past the prophecy. Her fingers were gentle as they leafed lovingly through each thin, blank page that followed, humbled by the beauty in the workmanship.

This was Áine, she thought with wonder. Myrddin said she put her essence and all her knowledge into The Book of Veils. The courage it must have taken, to consciously sacrifice your own future to ensure humanity's.

She was a little awed that she was related to someone so brave. Meru felt close to her ancestor, touching these pages. She imagined she could feel her presence in the room.

Thinking of how the book had responded when she'd asked for the prophecy, she smoothed out the page in front of her said, "Show me where The Cup of Inspiration is." She stared at the book for a few moments, her brow furrowing when she got no response.

"Do you know where The Cup of Inspiration is?" she tried. Fresh ink formed on the page.

The Cup of Inspiration vanished into the mist.

"Darn." Apparently it knew what Áine knew and nothing beyond that. She stared quietly for a heartbeat before she gave in to her curiosity.

"Tell me about the *Sauros*."

Sauros are an unnatural reptile/human hybrid
Created by Enlil, Lord of the Air,
During the height of the Sumerian civilization.
They were made to be
His personal guards and assassins.
Unable to follow
Any orders but those given by their creator.
Long lived and self-replicating,
Though easy to kill,
They contain the worst traits of both species.
No conscience, no remorse.

"Wow, this is better than my computer's search engine." Meru was a little worried she might become hysterical. This book was really freaking her out. And reading just a little bit like an Encyclopedia Mythica.

She'd learned a lot about Sumerian myth in her studies. Though she'd never heard of the *Sauros*, it had been an absolutely fascinating culture to study.

They were unusually advanced. Considered to be the first true civilization, though even they claimed to have replicated their empire from an older society. But it was the stories of their deities that had always held her interest the most.

Not only did the Sumerian gods "arrive" from the sky, in a similar story to the Tuatha Dé Danaan now that she thought of it, but they spent a lot of time creating, altering, and competing over the humans in their charge.

She'd never liked Enlil in any of those stories, liked him even less now that she knew he had been as real as he was evil. But she was rather fond of his brother, Enki. He was the "god" who'd saved humanity from the massive flood his brother caused when he'd decided to wipe the slate clean and destroy the population of Earth. How much of *that* myth was true?

She thought about what Myrddin had said about the *Sauros*. They followed only one Archon and the book told her that Archon was Enlil. Was he here now, in this time? Trying to stop them from fulfilling their prophecy so he could finish where he left off?

"Where is Enlil now?" Would Áine know that? It couldn't hurt to ask, she shrugged. And she really needed all the information she could get.

Enlil is where he has been for nearly five thousand years.
Imprisoned by his brother for his sins
In an inescapable darkness
Where every day is a hundred years
All the time in the world for regret.

"Whew." Her breath huffed out on a confused sigh. Now she was lost. If the *Sauros* only followed Enlil, but he was trapped in "inescapable darkness", then their actions just weren't adding up. Either Myrddin and Áine's book were wrong...or Enlil had somehow escaped.

She shivered. She needed to think about something else or she wouldn't be able to sleep for the nightmares. She'd never liked scary movies, they were more up Sheridan's alley. Give her a romantic comedy, even an action adventure any day over monsters or serial killers hiding in abandoned campgrounds.

Temptation reared its head. She hesitated for a moment, looking guiltily toward the door before leaning her chin in her hands and asking, "What is the difference between a werewolf and a Lycan?" Áine's talkative book immediately replied.

> *Werewolves are a natural evolution of the Therian species:*
> *Shifters,*
> *Part animal and part human,*
> *They live a relatively short life span*
> *Of three to five hundred years,*
> *Having both amazing healing capacity*
> *And the heightened instincts of their specific animal spirit.*
>
> *Lycans are faster healers,*
> *Harder to kill, nearly immortal.*
> *Cursed.*

"Holy Hannah." Her stomach clenched as the last word appeared. "Wait. What do you mean? You can't just say 'Lycans are cursed'. Why? How?" She waited impatiently as the writing appeared, too slowly in her opinion, on the following page.

> *Lycans were created by Zeus as his punishment*
> *For the blasphemous actions of King Lycaon of Arcadia.*
> *Lycaon was favored of Zeus*
> *Because he faithfully honored the god {see Archon} and so was protected,*
> *Though he was well known for being an evil and sadistic man,*
> *And much blood was shed under the banner of Zeus Lycaeus,*
> *Zeus the Wolf.*
> *When Lycaon found his wife had given birth to a son*
> *Which was not his, but the progeny of the god he had worshipped,*

He planned his revenge.
During a feast to honor Zeus,
Lycaon sacrificed the babe Nyctimus
Attempting to feed him to his own father.
When Zeus found out, he was enraged
He cursed all the men of Arcadia that very night
To become the animals they'd shown themselves to be.
Cursed to kill the things they loved.
Cursed for all time.

"I remember that story. And it's true? I always thought it was a little harsh. Cursing everyone because of one psycho king? Geesh. And I guess all the stories about Zeus having his hands in everybody's cookie jar have some basis in fact."

She rolled onto her back and thought about Damon. *Arkadios.* His last name made sense now. Damon "of Arcadia". "That's insane." She muttered, rolling back over to glance at the book once more. "That was over three thousand years ago."

"Three thousand, four hundred and sixty-six, to be exact." Meru screeched and leapt to her feet on the bed. She turned to find Damon standing beside the balcony door, arms folded casually as he leaned against the wall.

Meru swallowed audibly, holding a hand to her chest as she tried to catch her breath. "You scared me."

He raised one dark brow, his eyes cool. He straightened and walked over to the open book at the edge of the bed, reading the script that had appeared for her on the page.

"That is some inheritance Áine left for you."

She tilted her head, curious. "Did you know her?"

"I met her once or twice." He acknowledged. "Sheridan takes after her. Except for her smile. She had a beautiful smile.

Kind." He pierced her with a meaningful glance. "You have her smile."

Blushing at the praise, it took her a moment to notice how his eyes continued to be drawn to the pages below. "So you were there?" She gestured toward the story, taking a step closer to him, drawing his eyes back to her.

"Yes." He raked his hands through his hair, his only show of agitation. "I was there. Of course I was there. I was one of the King's fabled 'fifty sons'. Illegitimate son of a slave but still…a son."

Shock hit her hard. The Lycaon of myth was a spiteful, ferocious little man without honor. The polar opposite of the proud warrior who stood defensively before her.

"That …man was your father?"

Damon's hand slashed through the air.

"I did not say *that*. I said I was his son." Her heart bled for the anguish she heard in those simple words. He sat down beside the book, his back to her. It was only natural to kneel on the bed behind him and place her hand soothingly on his shoulder.

He had come here tonight because he'd had no choice. His obsession for her had only strengthened since this afternoon. He'd tasted heaven and he wanted…*needed* more.

The recon at Lily's house had only confirmed their original theory. He'd sniffed out the lingering presence of several *Sauros* and faint traces of the other two again.

Theron and Kyros. What in the name of Hades were *they* doing there? He'd hoped to find some of the *Dark* still loitering nearby, to question them if he could. But, no such luck.

For thousands of years, though still formidable, their enemies had been for the most part predictable.

The weakness of the *Dark*, whatever form they took, had always been arrogance. They believed they were on the side of right and power, believed they couldn't lose, making it easy to draw them out. But this…this was baffling.

Or maybe it was him. He couldn't seem to think clearly, worry, confusion and desire all warring with each other inside of him. All because of one tiny woman. Something dark and sinister was brewing on the wind. Myrddin's reactions, this prophecy all pointed to a scenario more dangerous than any the *Fianna* had faced since their formation. He had to be alert, on his toes to lead his men through this new challenge. And still, all he could think about when he returned was finding Meru. He found himself at her balcony doors again. He simply had no choice.

When he'd come in and realized what she was reading, he knew there was something else he had no choice but to do. He had to tell her the truth about what he was. Had to give her the freedom to reject him. He only hoped he could survive it when she did.

Chapter Seven

Damon began to tell her about the last day of his humanity and the memories flooded in, swamping him with images and emotions he had sealed away long ago.

He had seen twenty summers of backbreaking work, fought battles he didn't believe in and watched his mother age far too rapidly before his eyes.

Being the son of King Lycaon had brought him only suffering. He was determined that he and his mother would no longer suffer under the madman's yoke.

He walked on nimble feet down the large, airy hallways of his father's grand home, impatient to share his plan. His mother would be caring for the queen, as she had cared for the one who'd come before. The same servile job she'd had since she'd been stolen from her homeland. That is, he thought bitterly, when she wasn't being forced to share the king's bed.

The villa was in an uproar. Servants nervously rushing about, warriors standing in tight circles, tension and concern etched on their battle-scarred features.

It was unusual, he thought to himself as he walked past. The annual full moon celebration to honor Zeus Lycaeus, called The Feast of the Wolf, was usually a time of great revelry. The only time that the people of Arcadia were allowed to join the warriors and their king in drinking, dancing, and sacrificing to the ever bloodthirsty god.

It was also the perfect time to take his mother away from this dark, wretched place. He couldn't contain his smile of satisfaction, his mind turning inward once more as he made his plans.

"Kyros, my brother, do you smell that?"

"I do, Theron. What is that foul stench? It smells like rotting meat and dung."

"Indeed? All I smell is bastard."

He looked up to find the two eldest sons from the king's long-dead first wife standing arrogantly before him. In all these years, he had never understood the animosity they directed at him. It wasn't as if he were the only illegitimate child the king had sired. You couldn't throw a rock in Arcadia without hitting a product of Lycaon's fertile seed.

Regardless of that well-known fact, the pair had sought from early childhood to make his life more difficult.

They could not beat him in a fair fight. His mother came from the strong warrior stock of Eire, the good green land. Though his coloring left no doubt as to his paternity, her blood ensured that he was larger and stronger by far than the both of them put together.

So they sought their vengeance in other ways. Arranging it so that he was always chosen for the vilest labors. Having him beaten or whipped for each imagined slight or failure. Worst of all were the threatening taunts and dark insinuations pertaining to the treatment of his mother at their father's hands.

When he made a move to walk past them, Theron, the heir to his father's throne, stepped directly in his path. He stood several inches shorter than Damon, his muscles lean and wiry, his greasy hair hanging in his small, dark eyes.

Laying a hand on Theron could mean his death. He was too close to freedom to react rashly. He looked over his half brother's shoulder as the man pushed angrily closer, until he could feel his harsh breath on his face.

"Oh, how I wish it was your mother suffering that whore queen's fate tonight, and you that mewling babe Nyctimus."

Damon's gaze jerked up in confusion and Kyros, who'd been watching the byplay, began to laugh. He looked nearly identical to Theron, except for the thickening waistline that already spoke of royal overindulgence.

"That is too rich. The bastard has been too busy, up to his neck in animal waste, to know what goes on around him this night."

Kyros, ever the vicious gossip, filled him in on the discovery of the true sire of the queen's newborn child, as well as their father's volatile reaction.

"The faithless queen is, this very day, being sent to our warriors on the border. Given to them as a gift for their years of service. To be used by all and then sacrificed to the gods."

Damon paled. Theron leaned back to watch, obviously enjoying the moment.

"And the child?"

Kyros smiled, licking his lips grotesquely. "Nyctimus? Why, he is still here. In the kitchen last I saw him. Sliced and diced and seasoned to perfection for tonight's guest of honor."

Damon could not hold in his shout of surprised horror. "An innocent babe? The child of Zeus, no less? You have slaughtered the son of your god and you stand there laughing? Do you not fear His retribution?"

"We did nothing but watch the just and righteous actions of a true warrior and your Lord King!" Theron spit angrily. "How dare you, a filthy slave not good enough to breathe our air, deign to question him?"

Damon attempted to pull his outrage back in, overwhelmed by what he had heard. He looked stonily at Kyros. "Where is my mother?"

"She's being readied for tonight's celebration feast. Amazingly, she has been chosen to see to the King's pleasure. I'd personally be surprised if she lived through the night, with the mood our father is in this day."

He stepped forward quickly, only to be held back by several warriors who had moved to his side with Theron's nod.

"Patience, slave. You'll be able to see her tonight, as will all the peasants. We are all equal at The Feast of the Wolf, after all." And with a sneering laugh, he turned as the men pulled Damon out to the dusty yard beyond.

He looked in frustration at the high walls that kept his mother from him. She had been a warrior once, from a line of warriors, but her will had been beaten down over the years. He knew she did not have enough fight left to resist the king's violent advances.

A decision was made in that moment. He would return for her and take her away this night, but first he needed to right a horrifying wrong.

Making his way to the temple via the shadows, he did his best not to be seen. The people wandering by paid him no mind anyway. All thoughts were focused on the coming eve. No one had any idea of the nightmarish occurrences that had taken place within the king's walls.

Inside, the temple was empty and forbidding. He moved, swift and silent, to the hidden alcove he had watched the holy men enter so many times in the past.

He tried to quell his surprise that Zeus hadn't already arrived from his mountaintop home on Olympus, raining fire and death upon Lycaon for his grievous crimes. He hadn't come here to question a god, merely to right one unforgivable wrong. He could do no less.

The alcove hid a life-size statue of the father of the gods, Zeus himself. Damon went unerringly to the smoky orb in the figure's lowered left hand, touching it and calling Zeus' name. When he was younger and curious, he would peek behind the curtain as the priests sought advice or aid. He never had the nerve to find out what happened beyond this point. But this was an emergency.

At his call, the orb shone with a blazing light. Damon saw a flash from the corner of his eyes and then He was there. The young peasant kneeled in the presence of the handsomely bearded god.

"It seems Arcadia is impatient for my arrival." The booming voice greeted Damon cheerfully. His chin was raised by rough, surprisingly solid fingertips, the shining man smiling in recognition.

"You're the son of the painted warrior. That beauteous slave girl Lycaon is ever obsessed with." He chuckled as he straightened his robes impatiently.

"I cannot tell you how many times that man has asked for her devotion. But as you are no doubt aware, not even I can control the will of the heart. It truly rules us all."

Damon could not equate the man Zeus was describing, the besotted romantic, with the vicious murderer he knew his sire to be. He was simultaneously flooded with the inconceivable knowledge that the god standing jovially before him appeared to have *no idea* that his child had been killed, his lover sent to die. How could that be?

Bowing low before him, Damon relayed the news about Nyctimus and the queen, as well as King Lycaon's dastardly plans for the coming feast. The silence was deafening.

Damon looked up to see a rage unlike any he'd beheld before. Zeus looked at him, his strange eyes glowing with golden fire.

"Arcadia will pay." His threat hovered in the stale air of the temple as the god disappeared in a burst of light.

Damon stood, for a moment unsure if he had done the right thing. His mind flashed back to a scene only two days prior. The small, sweet-faced Nyctimus was being rocked in his own mother's arms.

"He has a great destiny ahead of him," she had crooned at the happy baby confidently. She'd had no idea it would arrive so quickly. Or that it would be covered in blood. No one, especially an innocent, deserved that end.

He rushed quickly toward his room in the slave's quarters, eager to gather the trade goods he had painstakingly hoarded in anticipation of this day. He would take his mother back to her homeland. They would finally be free.

That was the last thought he had before feeling a bone shattering pain against his temple. Through the roaring in his ear drums, he heard Theron's wicked laugh. And then…nothing.

When his eyes had opened again, at first it seemed he was trapped in a nightmare. He was tied against a wooden pillar in the king's great hall, where the slaves who were of no more use or prisoners of war were usually tied to be mocked and ridiculed before being taken out to the altar stone and sacrificed to Zeus.

There was blood dripping down his face. He almost missed the piercing screams around him due to the throbbing pain in his head.

He blinked away the sweat and blood from his eyes and immediately wished he hadn't. His imagination had never fashioned a nightmare this terrible. Men writhing on the floor, screaming in agony with no apparent cause. Women frozen in terror beside them. And above them all was Zeus. He hovered over the tortured masses of twisting flesh, wrath incarnate. His body, a beacon of fury, the storm of lightning and judgment from which there could be no escape.

"Arcadia, for your crimes you will not have an easy death." His voiced echoed over the wailing masses.

"Instead, I give to you a gift. The banner of war you so easily wave, the ravenous wolf that fills those near and far with terror and revulsion…wear it with pride for all eternity."

The obvious agony of the men around Damon increased and he, as well, began to feel a rippling, burning sensation whipping through his flesh.

"The name Lycaon, Lycan, will be forever the brand of an evil that all of mankind will hunt and seek to destroy. Named for your cowardly dog of a king!"

Damon could not contain his scream of pain as he felt the rope that tied him fray apart with his body's change. He watched his hands as the flesh wavered, grew larger, more grotesque. Black fur sprouted like needles through his skin and claws grew from the beds of his bloodied nails.

"As for Arcadia's women and children, by your own hand you will grant me retribution this night. The devil within you will leave you no choice. Your women for my woman. Your children for my child!"

Damon felt the beast stir within him, straining to attack, and held it back with a sheer force of will. In his mind, a screaming voice kept demanding him to search for his mother.

He pushed through the crowds of hair-covered beasts. His shimmering eyes took in the fanged, drooling monsters as they ravaged their prey in a mad frenzy, ripping out the throats of every female, every babe in sight.

Smells and sounds bombarded him from every direction. He could hear the screaming in the streets, could smell the strange, sweet aroma of the blood as it filled the hall.

Beneath the other odors, he caught his mother's scent. He knew it better than his own and he vigorously renewed his efforts to cross the giant hall to her side.

What he saw then would haunt his dreams for thousands of years. His mother lay still, her clothing torn, blood pouring from the bite just delivered to her shoulder.

Lycaon, looking like a crazed, mindless animal, was thrusting on top of her roughly, chanting her name over and over in a deep garbled voice around his blood soaked fangs.

Damon's vision went red with rage as he leapt on the beast, ripping him from his mother's broken form. Lycaon struggled for a moment, until his gaze caught on and were riveted to the sight of the woman on the ground, her life blood pumping quickly out to soak into the dirt floor.

His horrified expression clashed with Damon's for a moment, then the cursed king was kneeling on the ground, his arms open in invitation. His howl of grief resonated through the maddened crowd.

Damon didn't hesitate. With the knowledge of the beast he had become, he punched through the king's chest with a clawed fist, crushing his heart to sand. He reared back with an angry roar, swiping the sharp daggers across the waiting throat, severing the head completely from its shoulders.

Ignoring the outraged bellows behind him, he lifted his dying mother in his arms and ran.

Through the narrow streets of Arcadia, where the blood ran free. Through farmed fields and rocky hillsides. Even as he'd felt the change reverse and his human legs grow weary, he continued forward.

He ran all night beneath the mocking glow of the moon until he reached the shore where the ships of the traders were moored. Laying his mother on the pure white sand, he listened to her dying words.

She had held on as long as she could, but she knew she wouldn't make it home alive. She asked that her body be taken to the shores of Eire and burned there. Damon agreed huskily, his heart in his throat.

He told her what he'd done, how he'd informed Zeus of the king's treachery and asked for her forgiveness, which she immediately gave. She asked him to forgive his father but he could not.

"He was not a good man and he deserved to be punished," she choked out, obviously in tremendous pain. "But I know that he loved me, as well as someone like he knew how." And with those last words, tearing his soul to pieces, she died.

He'd had wrapped her in a blanket and carried her body onto the nearest trading vessel, intimidating the captain into granting them passage and him some covering for the long journey.

The captain had recognized Damon's resemblance to the terrifying King of Arcadia, so he didn't question Damon's request to have himself locked in the tiny hold for the length of the voyage.

The slave he sent to feed him each day often came back looking shaken, as if he'd seen a ghost, but he'd never said a word in complaint. And the captain never asked, lest the wrath of that bloodthirsty maniac Lycaon fall upon his head.

When they'd arrived in his mother's homeland, Damon burned her body on the beach as she'd requested. Then he turned and headed into the woods, as deep as he could go, where he couldn't hurt any passersby should he change again.

He wasn't sure how long he existed there in his limbo of grief and fury. Years spent cursing himself, cursing his father, cursing Zeus. He learned that strong emotions triggered his beast. He discovered that his appetite, as well as myriad other senses, had increased dramatically.

He subsisted on the animals of the forest and he shied away from any possible encounter with the few villagers who braved the darkened wood. After several bitter years, when he caught the scent of a stranger in his territory, his loneliness and curiosity compelled him to seek out the source.

The distinctly unusual aroma told him that there was something unique…powerful, about this man dressed in the robes of the spiritual leaders his mother had described, when she'd tell him about her people in a voice tinged with longing. His instincts told him the sage could be trusted.

Myrddin knew all about Damon and what he'd gone through. He'd listened in disbelief as the elder had told him the truth about the gods he had worshipped, their fallibility and their deception.

The wise man offered to teach him to control the untamed thing inside him. Said he would train him to use his curse to help the innocent. Those who fell victim to creatures just as deadly as he. Seeing it as a chance for redemption, a chance to honor his brave mother's memory, Damon had agreed. And the rest? Well, the rest was history.

Chapter Eight

He blinked away the memories and turned, surprised to feel Meru's face pressed against the back of his neck, shoulders shaking. He knew she wasn't laughing this time. He felt her tears soak into the collar of his shirt.

Damon slid her around from behind his back to his lap in one smooth maneuver, wrapping her up and rocking her in his arms as she cried. She humbled him, this compassionate, generous, amazing woman.

She slid under his iron-plated defenses as if they were made of cobwebs and air. Decimated his control, dissolved his anger. It made him feel all too human…when he was anything but.

"I'm so sorry." She sniffled, rubbing her nose with the sleeve of her pajama top, looking sweetly adorable. Eyes as blue as the ocean looked into his, moisture threatening to spill once more, tangling in her curled up lashes.

Such simple words, said with honest sincerity, and he felt the dark hole inside him mend a little, healed by the light that was Meru.

He kissed away the tear that had fallen to her cheek, tasting the warm salt of it on his tongue. She looked at him, silent apart from her sniffles, before turning her other cheek toward him for similar treatment. He willingly obliged, holding her close as she snuggled deeper into his lap.

Tenderness. That was the emotion twisting his heart. And something more. Something he knew, but wasn't ready to acknowledge, even to himself.

He wasn't sure how long he sat there, easing them both with his gentle rocking motions, before he became aware of a few important details.

The first being that the squeezes and pats they had been offering each other in comfort had turned into caresses laden with sensual undertones. Her hand on his shoulder, running down his arm, making his blood heat.

The second was her scent. His nose nuzzled against the curls at her temple, intoxicated by the warm, arousing fragrance that he now knew he'd recognize anywhere. She responded by placing her lips at the base of his throat and inhaling blissfully before reaching up to plant a soft, closed-mouth kiss on the cleft of his shadowed chin.

The final, and possibly most critical, detail he noted as their gazes clashed was the delayed awareness of something it shamed him, as a man, to have missed.

"You're not wearing underwear."

She arched an eyebrow, an impish little smile formed on her full, pink lips. "Nope."

"I should go." Rather than moving away, he held her a bit tighter. Meru, an expression of true bewilderment replacing her grin, leaned back to look him square in the eye.

She had no doubt he was aroused. Not only because of the proof currently making its presence happily known against her hip but also from the heated expression in his darkening eyes.

But she also saw worry there. Caution.

As he'd told her about his traumatic past, she'd been overcome with despair for all that he'd been through, all that he'd suffered. She'd also come to several stunning realizations.

She was in love with Damon Arkadios. How else could she explain her awareness of him, the powerful pull he had on her? She'd never leapt without looking as Lily did, though she wasn't as cynical as Sheridan. But this, the way she felt about him…it was easy. It was right. As if she'd always known him, always loved him.

She realized why he had been so careful to assure her of his control, even at the height of passion…*especially* then. He was afraid he would hurt her. Afraid his own feelings would overwhelm him and he would become no better than his father.

Damon would rather die than cause her the slightest discomfort. There was no doubt in her mind. Not because she had any romantic delusions that he had fallen as quickly as she had but because of the kind of man he was.

A protector. A guardian. *Fianna*. A sexy, wonderful man. And she was determined to prove it to him.

New to the art of seduction, she sent a quick prayer to her new best friend, Danu, that she didn't send him screaming, or laughing, in the other direction.

She smiled up at him from beneath her lashes and gently pulled herself from his arms. He looked at her, his suspicion evident as she stood beside the bed, her knees brushing his, her hand fiddling with the hem of her top.

Sliding her fingers up to the top button of the white cotton top, she twirled it to and fro before releasing the catch. She saw his throat work as he swallowed hard, she had his full attention.

"So that's one vote for leaving." She murmured as she moved on to the second button in the line, releasing it quickly and moving on to the third and fourth. "And one vote for staying."

She glanced quickly at his eyes, smiling in secret delight as she noted how focused he was on the small patch of skin revealed by her impromptu striptease.

If her actions were affecting him, that was nothing compared to the havoc they were wreaking on her. Her breasts had begun to tingle, aware as never before of the scrape of the cloth against her tightening nipples. Her fingers trembled and fumbled with the buttons as she felt his attention, riveted on her, arousing her to a fever pitch.

She pressed her legs together, her hips rocking in a slight, sultry sway to the music in her head. She lifted her fingers from their task to caress her skin along the edge of the fabric. Wetness gathered between her thighs at the deep, warning rumble that came from his chest.

Reaching the fifth and final button, she stood poised for a moment, enjoying his anticipation before shrugging her shoulders, the top sliding to the floor. Suddenly she was worried about his reaction. All her old insecurities about her generous figure rose to the surface. Diving for the bed covers sounded more and more tempting.

"Can I change my vote?" he grated harshly, the muscles in his neck taut, his hands fisted against his thighs in restraint. She took one step back when he made a move as if to reach for her.

"It'll cost you." She brazened it out, distracting him by motioning to his clothing. "We do have a very specific dress code." He flashed a devilish grin before standing to tower over her.

"I do believe my ability to remove my clothes in an entertaining fashion has been questioned." She chuckled softly at his words, remembering their conversation on the dance floor that first night. The laughter died in her throat as he began to unbutton his shirt.

His dark eyes scorched her skin as he revealed his body slowly, sensually. He toed off his boots and reached for the clasp on his pants, and she was sure she might actually swoon. He was *good*. She'd been right. He could have made a fortune.

Making sure she was watching, he bit his lower lip and slid down the zipper. Moments later he stood, tossing the pants in a heap on the floor, completely naked.

Her mouth parted on a panting moan as her gaze traveled over the rippling mass of corded muscles now bared to her gaze. Her throat closed and a shiver of delicious trepidation skitter down her spine at the sheer size of him.

He took a determined step toward her and she stepped back once more, hands raised. His nostrils flared at the action, his eyes narrowed in warning.

"You're playing a dangerous game, Meru." His rasping voice slid down her spine in a rough caress and she shivered. "If you act like prey, the predator in me will want to run you down."

He thought he was warning her, she thought a little wildly. In reality, his words went off like volcanic explosions throughout her body. Her nipples hardened to diamond points, her already dripping pussy pulsing in need, ready for him.

"Promises, promises." He looked ready to pounce at her husky words, so she spoke up quickly.

"Damon, please. This afternoon was the hottest, most incredible experience of my life. I only have one regret." He tilted his head in question. "I didn't get to see you. To touch you and taste you the way you did me."

She saw him still, his white-knuckled fists clenched at his side. Damon's eyes closed for a moment before nodding sharply, turning toward the bed and gifting Meru with clear view of his incredible backside.

He carefully closed the book and placed it on the bedside table. She watched as he reclined on the bed, his back supported by the pillows against the headboard, his nude body displayed for her pleasure. And he waited.

Happy Birthday to me. She let out a lustful sigh. Her present was definitely worth the wait. She looked at his reclining form and marveled at the massive proportions of perfection that made up this man.

My man, her body said adamantly. Her logical mind was too busy ogling the eye candy to argue.

She wondered how someone so big could move so gracefully. And he was big. Everywhere. He sprawled out on her silk coverlet, his frame taking up half the bed, skin like dark velvet on steel. A larger than life personification of sex and sin. Her eyes lingered over the black swirls of hair around his chest and navel, begging for her touch, before they lowered, giving in to irresistible temptation.

She had never considered that part of a man's body particularly attractive. Granted, she'd never seen one this up close and personal. But she thought she'd seen enough to make an informed decision. She had been wrong. It was a work of art.

The thick length of his cock lay heavy against his muscled abs and she felt a little faint at the sight. How on earth had that fit inside her?

The object of her fascination was hard and taut, the veins clearly outlined on the flushed shaft, the tip of the wide, crowned head already weeping with arousal.

She licked her lips, her mouth watering, the desire to taste him as he had tasted her a carnal need. To make him as wild as she had been. Wild for her.

A deep, delicious rumble came from the direction of the bed and she dragged her eyes upward with difficulty. Damon was a study in restraint. His biceps bulged as his fists held the gold and emerald bedspread beneath his hips in a white knuckled death grip. His torso seemed to strain toward her, black eyes lava hot as they studied her naked frame.

She knew she was a hypocrite, but she felt very insecure. The perfection of his body highlighted the flaws of her own. She lifted her arms to cover her nakedness, though she didn't seem to have enough arm for the job. Damon wasn't amused.

"Don't hide from me, Meru. I need to see you too." He saw the embarrassment on her face and the rumbling in his chest grew louder.

"Don't you know how sexy you are? How hard you make me?" He leaned back, his voice low and husky as he gripped his thick erection in his fist. Meru watched, hypnotized, as he began to stroke himself, his fingers sliding through the pearly liquid leaking from the head of his cock.

"You do this to me. Only you." Up and down, twisting roughly, his hips pumping up from the bed as she watched. He groaned and her fascinated gaze jumped to his face. Tight with need, almost savage in its beauty, his look seared her through to her core, her own hips thrusting slightly, already imagining the feel of him inside her, filling her.

"Come closer, baby, and touch me. I need your hands on me. I'm craving the taste of those lush breasts. Longing to stick my tongue up that creamy, delicious pussy and eat you alive, your thighs draped over my shoulders. To fill my hands full of your sweet curves as I make you scream."

She trembled like a leaf in a storm, unaware that she was shuffling closer toward him, mesmerized by the erotic pictures he was painting.

"I can hold off if you need me to. Control the need to pin you down and fuck you, hard and fast like I'm dying to, but not for much longer. Just imagining your soft hands on my skin, your mouth stretched wide around my aching cock…"

She closed her eyes on a moan. The man said the dirtiest, sexiest things. His words flooded her system like a drug.

Her eyes popped open seconds later, stunned that she had gotten close enough to the bed for him to wrap his large, hot hands around her wrists.

His face was so tight with lust that she was sure he would make good on his words to take her quickly. And she was too turned on to object, all her insecurity forgotten. She just knew she needed him any way he wanted to take her.

Damon didn't attack her. He pulled her up onto the bed beside him instead, gentling his grip on her wrists as he placed her palms against his heated chest. "Touch me." It was a gruff demand. Damon leaned his head back against the wooden frame as if in pain.

Her hands shook with need. He was so warm, his skin as velvety as she imagined, as hard as she'd known it would be.

"Well, since you asked so nicely." Her husky chuckle caused Damon to shift impatiently beside her.

She explored the textures of his body, fingers tangling and tugging teasingly in his chest hair, sliding over the broad expanse of his shoulders, the flexing muscles of his stomach. She leaned closer, inhaling.

He smelled of dark woods and freedom. The male musk that surrounded him, unique to him, was intoxicating.

Her breath puffed against his tightening nipple, her pink tongue lightly licking in query. His whole body jerked and she heard a slight cracking sound, which she ignored in favor of his other nipple. The flat disk beaded against her lips and he arched under her again as she nipped at his flesh.

A thrilling feeling of power rushed through her. He wanted her. Needed her. She placed warm, open-mouthed kisses down his torso, nibbling on his ribs, dipping her tongue into that elusive navel. His skin burned against her lips and she could hear his breath catch each time her tongue touched his flesh.

As her head slowly lowered to his engorged cock, it appeared to move on its own, seeming to reach up and beg for her touch. Her eyes rose up in surprise to the man on the bed beside her, his hands clasping the headboard behind him, his chest rising like a bellows as he struggled for breath.

He gave a closed mouthed smile at her curious expression, she knew he was trying not to frighten her by revealing the emerging fangs lancing his gums...but she saw them.

She felt another gush of arousal flood her sex at the sight, at this proof of his fraying control. His groan drew her fascinated gaze away from his mouth, swirling eyes begging her to continue what she'd been doing.

Quickly absorbed in her task once more, she studied the liquid glistening from the slit, dripping down the shaft of his erection. She breathed deeply, taking in the dark, earthy scent of his arousal.

She was so turned on she could feel the hard, pounding pulse of her clit and she squeezed her thighs together tightly. Her lips parted as she watched his cock jerk toward her once more, demanding her undivided attention.

She was suddenly very glad that she liked to read erotic fiction. She desperately wanted to please him, wanted to put all her reading to good use.

One hand gently cupped the tight sac of his hair-roughened balls as she licked the flushed head with delicate laps of her tongue, curiously needy for the taste of him.

Damon's hips gave a small helpless twitch before stilling, as if the added sensation was too much. "This may not be such a smart—oh baby, that's feels so *good*!"

Inspired by his reaction and his instantly addicting flavor, she laved his entire shaft with her tongue before trying to wrap her lips around him. He was so thick and long that she could only fit half of him in her mouth. She closed her fist around the lower part of his cock, licking and sucking as much as she could reach in vigorous delight.

His reaction was gratifying. His groan poured over her, nearly drowning out the sound of cracking, crumbling wood that signaled the demise of a small section of the headboard behind him.

One large hand reached down to caress her hair, soft as a butterfly's wing. Her curls tangled on something sharp and she knew he was trying not to scratch her with his newly emerged claws.

Reaching up, she placed one hand over his, keeping him there as she licked the sensitive flesh around the base of the crown, pressing her tongue against the vein there, smiling slightly as he arched against her mouth with a growl. She breathed out slowly as she relaxed her jaw muscles to take him as deep into her mouth as she could.

His cock hit the back of her throat and she instinctively swallowed, Damon nearly leapt from the bed in reaction.

"*Oh shit*, Meru…damn, *how did you*—? Oh gods, *yes!*"

His clawed grip on her hair tightened convulsively as he pumped himself lightly into her waiting mouth. "That feels— oh, suck my cock, baby. Yes, just like *that*."

She felt the lightest sprinkling of soft fur on the back of his hand and shuddered with delight, pressing it against her head harder in a mute plea for him to let go of his restraint. His paw-like fist clenched in her hair, tugging her head up and her mouth away from its new favorite treat.

"You don't know what you're asking for," he growled. "I don't want to hurt you." She pulled against the restraining hand, extending her tongue to swipe at his pulsing shaft.

Her eyes rose, looking straight into his. "You would never hurt me." Her voice held absolute knowledge. Total trust. And he went wild.

She was pulled up and flipped onto her back in the middle of the gigantic bed before she could blink, Damon was kneeling before her spread thighs.

His smile was tight, as if he were still trying to reassure her even through his need. His sharp white fangs gleamed in the softly lit room. The only other outward changes she could see was the slight thickening of the furlike hair already covering his chest and forearms, the muscles of his already impressive torso rippling, growing larger and more pronounced. It was obvious he still held back from completely changing but she was in no way disappointed.

She could feel her moisture pooling on the silk beneath her. He was the sexiest thing she'd ever seen. Still Damon, just…more.

Her confidence in her own safety made her bold. Gripping his neck with surprising strength, she pulled him down for a deep, open-mouthed kiss. She wrapped her tongue enticingly around the sharp, sexy points of his teeth before sucking his lower lip into her mouth and nipping playfully.

Damon pulled back, shock and lust stamped across his expression. He shuddered, his cock brushing against her wet pussy. Her hips twisted beneath him, begging him for more. She reached for him but he gripped her arms and raised them above her head with a silent order to leave them where they lay. He slid down her body until his mouth was poised over her dampened curls. Tilting her hips up high, he licked his full lower lip and breathed her in deeply.

"The Lycan sense of smell is truly an amazing thing." He took another breath. "I caught your scent that first night and knew I wanted to taste." Her eyes grew bigger.

"Then I tasted this delectable pussy and knew I would never get enough." He growled hotly, vibrating the curls so close to his mouth.

"What do I smell like?" Her gasping question made him close his eyes in need, his clawed hands curving on her silken skin.

"Like flowers and spice. When you're aroused, the scent grows stronger, tempting me, drowning me." He licked the alluring, dew-covered curls lightly, placing his hands on her thighs to spread her wide open to his gaze.

"And your taste." He hummed appreciatively. "It's addictive. Delicious. Thick, sweet cream that I don't think I'll ever get enough of."

She cried out hoarsely as he ended the conversation by diving down into her wet heat, tasting her fully with firm strokes of his rough, clever tongue.

Her hips arched upward, already close, almost desperate. He took her drenched folds in his mouth, sucking and licking each in turn, before sucking on her clit with a strong, steady pressure, causing her to come in a shocking rush.

That seemed to be what he was waiting for, she thought, feeling him chuckle against her flesh before thrusting his long tongue deep inside. He swirled it around aggressively, greedily lapping up all of her juices and demanding more.

She came again and again against his avid mouth, his thick, thrusting fingers, crying out his name on a plea to stop. A plea to never stop. Tugging on his hair in an attempt to ease this pleasure that bordered on pain.

After one last, savoring lick, Damon climbed back up her body, her thighs still caught in his firm grip. He pushed her legs up until her knees bent close to her shoulders, her thighs brushing the sensitive tips of her breasts.

Looking lustfully at the bounty before him, her cream glinted wetly on his chin. He licked his lips as she watched, his smile pure carnality. He took his rigid cock in hand and entered her slick channel in one long, powerful stroke. She arched beneath him, crying out at the hot stretch of her flesh. He was so big. And it felt so good.

He growled. "You're mine."

She nodded jerkily at his rough decree.

His ministrations had left her so wet that he slid in more easily than he had that first time, though it was still a tight fit. She watched him throw his head back in ecstasy at the feel of her muscles contracting around him, pulling him deeper.

"That's it, Meru, Take it. Take all of me. *Yes.*"

Damon's positioning left her completely open to him, each slow, controlled thrust filling her up, touching her core. She looked at his face, finding his eyes blazing down at the spot where their bodies joined, and hers followed.

It was a beautiful sight. His dark cock wet with her arousal, stretching her open, going impossibly deep.

"*Damon*," she moaned, reaching for his hips to pull him more fully against her, needing more of him, straining to thrust against him from her helpless position.

He wasn't about to rush this time. He filled her again and again, slow and deep, despite her moaned demands for him to go faster. Tears of frustration and mindless pleasure spilled down her cheeks as her head whipped back and forth against the pillows.

He seemed to sense each time she was close to coming. He would slow down just enough or move in just the right way to leave her dangling on the edge, in desperate need of satisfaction.

Unable to take it anymore, the control he held even partially shifted, she reached between her bent legs to touch him. She gently caressed his ball sac where it sat high and taut against his skin.

He growled.

Then, straining to wrap her fingers around the base of his thick cock as it slid back from her body, using her own moisture as lubricant, she squeezed firmly as he slid through her snug fist and into her even tighter pussy. She was determined to throw him off balance. She needed to come. *Now*.

He seemed to arrive at the same conclusion a heartbeat later, her name a barely recognizable roar on his lips as he slammed his hips forward, pounding into her wildly.

Her legs slid around his waist, clinging to him as he fell on her breasts, sucking her deeply into his mouth, still careful not to break the skin. She arched into his mouth, the scrape of his fangs against her sensitive flesh sending bolts of white hot lust up her spine.

Shaking the bed with his powerful thrusts, he groaned against her flesh, licking roughly up the curve of her breast to the pulse beat at her neck, his breath hot and humid against her.

She was climbing higher than she'd ever been, higher than she ever imagined she could go. He reared away from her throat, taking her mouth desperately with his own, rubbing against her clit with every angled stroke.

She soared, her whole body in flames. His cock swelled impossibly inside her as her inner walls milked his length, demanding that he join her in her flight.

He ate her cries and fed her his own as he shot hotly into her, jerking against her as he felt his soul ripping through his cock to merge with hers. He came long and hard, jets of heat lashing up his spine again and again, his body reshaping itself, his mind transforming, knowing that something within him had changed.

From the moment he'd held her in his arms, from the moment they'd met, it had already begun. And now he knew he could no longer avoid the truth.

He was in love. He was still terrified at his lack of control around her but thankfully not as much as before. Hadn't she seen him partially changed and still reached for him with acceptance and desire? Hadn't he managed to pull the beast back before he'd had a chance to bite the fragile flesh of her shoulder, to taste her blood as he'd longed to do?

As he lay down beside her, scooping her sleepy body up to cuddle her against him, he felt a renewed sense of hope. He would protect her, aid her in her quest and hold her as long as he could. As long as he held back from completely losing himself to the desires of the wolf, she could be safe. And his.

Chapter Nine

I'm dreaming.

Again.

She felt the cool, damp grass beneath her, smelled the sweet lavender on the breeze, even shivered at the slight chill in the air. It all felt incredibly real. But she knew it was a dream.

Meru stood and looked around, recognizing the scene from the last dream she'd had. The same ethereal landscape, the same deep green mound beside the same flowing stream that threaded through the landscape like a ribbon of sky.

"Hello, Meru, daughter of Áine."

She turned to see the familiar woman once again standing beside her. She seemed somehow a part of the mystical land that surrounded them. Her eyes were the clear blue of the water babbling beside them, her dress the same emerald green as the hillside. Her hair seemed radiant as the sun, the daylight glinting off the white flowers that glittered in the strands as if a jeweled crown had been woven in the flaxen tresses.

"Danu." Meru breathed reverently. The True Queen smiled kindly and took her hand, lacing it through her own as she began walking beside the water's edge.

"It's so lovely here." Meru sighed. She noticed a large, modern house situated at the edge of the woods across the water. It was all windows and thick timber beams, with a wide deck meant for enjoying the enchanting view. It should have seemed out of place here but it was perfect. She wondered if Danu lived there.

"You'll have to come home soon. I have so missed your family." At her questioning glance, Danu shook her head, abruptly changing the topic.

"Do you know why you're here?"

Meru knew what she was referring to. "The Cup of Inspiration. The one you created for Áine. Can you tell me where it is?"

"Only you, my Druid daughter, can find the answer to that. What I *can* tell you is where it went when it disappeared from Áine and that silver-eyed Archon's sight."

Meru heard an interesting note in Danu's voice when she mentioned Myrddin. The way she said Archon as if it were a bad taste in her mouth confused her. For some reason, she had just assumed Danu was an Archon as well, like the rest of the Tuatha.

"The Tuatha Dé Danaan are *not* Archon!" Danu responded to her unspoken thought almost angrily. Meru felt the wind pick up around them, lifting her dark curls with the force of Danu's emotions.

"The Tuatha were the first to arrive in this dimension, pilgrims seeking a land to love and nurture, far away from the power hungry violence of the Archons. But the portal could not be completely closed behind them. The others soon followed, seeking more territory to conquer."

Her hand tightened on Meru's arm with remembered frustration, but her voice softened as she continued. "I gave the Tuatha gifts to protect themselves, hide them from prying eyes. But I could not hide the native inhabitants of this world I had discovered."

It was clear to see that Danu blamed herself for all the tragedy and subjugation her dimension had inflicted on Earth. And also obvious that she had no love for the Archon race or its council.

Meru squeezed Danu's arm comfortingly, causing her to smile and return the affectionate embrace.

"It's all right, Meru. And I don't hate all Archons. Truth be told, I don't hate any of them. They are just misguided. There are even one or two, our friend Myrddin for example, whose philosophies still align with ours. He is a good man. I am glad he's finally going to find some happiness and love of his own. Especially after that horrible debacle with his brother's wife."

Realizing she was confusing Meru, Danu just laughed softly and shrugged. "I am wandering away from the topic at hand. It is just so nice to be able to talk directly with someone again. It has been a long time. I was going to tell you of the Cup."

Meru listened, entranced by the lovely woman and her musical voice as she explained. "Myrddin spoke to you of The Book of Veils, how Áine put her essence into the book, giving up her life as priestess and leader of her people to ensure that all she had learned would be ready for you when the time was right." At Meru's nod, Danu continued.

"That is the way of powerful Magick. There is always a price to be paid. The gifts I created for the Tuatha have cost me dearly. The Cup of Inspiration was no different. The loss of Áine wasn't the only sacrifice needed to make it, but it was, for me, the hardest."

Danu looked off into the distance. "When you create a power-filled object like that, infuse it with a piece of your spirit, the thing you have made often takes on a life, and a Magick, all its own."

She looked deeply into Meru's eyes. "I did not make Áine's Cup disappear, it left of its own accord, searching for the next person who could call it forth.

I created it specifically to grant the gift of knowing to Áine, her unique genetic markers. Her spirit. I ensured that no hands, Archon or *Other*, not even a member of my own Tuatha Dé Danaan, could touch it. And no mere human who held it would know it was more than an earthen goblet."

Danu sighed. "The ability to gain absolute knowledge, on any topic you request, would be far too dangerous a weapon if it were to fall into the wrong hands. One black-hearted question could unmake this dimension. But there has never been one more selfless, more loving or more aware of the responsibilities of her power than your ancestor."

She turned away from Meru and looked out across the vast green landscape. "When I realized what Áine had seen with my gift, I understood that it would go next to a woman of her direct genetic line, someone who shared her spirit of compassion and wisdom. And here you are at last."

Meru was amazed by the information she'd just been given. But she still had no idea where to even begin searching for the elusive chalice.

"It will come to you. Trust yourself."

Meru felt a sudden, strange breeze wrap around her. Her limbs grew heavy and her body filled with embarrassing heat. Danu looked on, her smile knowing.

"Enjoy your mate, daughter of Áine. Guard him as he will guard you against the danger that is coming." She turned as if to walk away, her image near fading as the landscape began to blur before Meru's fluttering eyes. She swung back around, calling out as if from a distance.

"And don't forget to tell Myrddin that the answer to his riddle lies in his past. In his weakness for a fickle heart."

Thoroughly baffled by the cryptic statement, barely able to concentrate for the intensely pleasurable waves of lust rolling over her body, the scene changed as Meru came to sudden awareness.

It was morning. She was awake, her body writhing on the luxurious Egyptian cotton sheets of her giant bed, her head burrowing into the softness of her pillow. Another head, covered in black, silken hair, was nuzzling into the already damp cradle of her sex.

She opened one sleep-filled, incredulous eye to find Damon nestled comfortably between her thighs, as if he'd settled in for the duration. He was bringing her to full wakefulness with his hot, amazingly talented mouth.

"Again?" Breathless disbelief filled her voice. They'd turned to each other several times throughout the long night, both insatiable in their need for the other.

He felt the tensing of her thighs and looked up with a sinful grin of greeting. "I couldn't resist." His voice rumbled in that sexy, scratchy way that had her squirming beneath him.

"I woke up to the smell of you, the feel of you around me. I had to have more." He said the last on a rough growl before returning to his previous efforts with a diligence that had her arching on a groan.

He lapped up her cream like a man starved, his broad tongue scraping against her sensitive tissues, the sensation enough to start her trembling.

Damon lifted his head until only his heated breath touched her needy pussy, his thick fingers slipping easily through her wetness, parting her until she was opened fully to his view.

"I love looking at you. All pink and sweet, swollen and wet just for me." He stared down at her so intently that she shifted her hips against the bed, uncomfortable and aroused by his focus at the same time.

His shoulders pressed her thighs wide as he flicked her clit with delicate precision, the fingers of one hand gathering her juices and spreading them lower, making Meru jerk in surprise.

"*Let me.*" He growled in dark desire, his tongue thrusting deeply into her flooding pussy, his lips nipping and sucking, eating at her with delicious desperation.

Focused on the searing ecstasy boiling through her veins, she didn't realize what he had planned until she felt one wet, blunt-edged finger push firmly into her tingling ass. The puckered hole clenched forcefully around the digit, the feeling completely foreign. Undeniably erotic.

Damon moaned in pleasure, enjoying her reaction. She instinctively pushed against him, taking him deeper before arching forward against his mouth.

She was drowning in the dual edge of sharp sensation. Never in her life would she have imagined allowing any man *that* particular intimacy. She couldn't fathom it being a pleasurable experience for anyone. And yet here she was, pumping her backside against his finger, reveling in the tingling, burning pressure.

"So fucking tight." He panted between greedy licks. "You're squeezing my finger like a vise, Meru. You like it, don't you? I can't wait to sink my cock inside, to fuck your luscious ass." He felt the shocked tensing of her muscles as she registered his words and he laughed huskily, fingers still thrusting slowly inside her.

"Soon, baby, but not this time. This time I want back inside that hot pussy. After you come around my tongue, feed me some more of that sweet cream, I want to feel you wrapped around my cock." He followed his hot promise with action, his head dipping down to suck her clit hard, lapping at her juices, devouring her.

It was too much. The teasing licks, pumping finger and debauched words all combined to throw her over the edge. She heard herself scream his name as she shattered. Splintering into a million pieces that shot like stars into the atmosphere.

She heard Damon snarl and glanced down to see a look of agonized pleasure on his face as he rooted deeply, drinking down her release as if it were the finest ambrosia.

Still trembling, she tried to clear her muddled thoughts and focus on him. She wanted to feel him inside her again. Tugging on his shoulders, she called his name. "Damon?"

It took two more tries, her fingers pulling his head up by his hair for him to stop feasting and lift his head. His dazed eyes had darkened in the now familiar way. Light glimmered within the swirling ebony, causing her just sated body to shiver once again with need.

She jerked on his hair with a laugh as he attempted to return to the warmth between her thighs. Finally he focused in on her face. She would have sworn he was pouting.

"Get up here and roll on your back." She couldn't believe that was her voice making demands. Neither, apparently, could Damon. He raised one eyebrow at her comment, a smile breaking through the lust etched on his features.

She blushed, but held his stare until he lifted himself slowly, his arms bulging with power as he raised himself up on the bed, his body brushing suggestively against hers the entire way.

He held himself over her, his lips inches from her own, his erection jerking against her thigh in excitement. She could feel the drops of pre-cum beading on the head of his cock, rubbing into her burning flesh.

Damon seemed to be tamping down on his need to dominate, biting his lip carefully around the elongating canines that glinted at her as he grinned crookedly.

Placing her palms against his shoulders, she smiled sweetly into his glorious face…and pushed. A whoosh of sound left him as he landed heavily beside her and she quickly scampered over his large body to straddle his hips.

"You really are a bad girl, aren't you, baby?" Damon chuckled at her show of force, his tone telling her he liked it.

"Maybe you're just a bad influence."

She was flooded with a rush of feminine power, of desire, in this new position. Until now, it seemed he had always taken her as she lay in one helpless, twisted position after another, unable to do anything other than submit. Not that she didn't enjoy submitting, she thought with an inward smile.

He was long and hard, pulsing behind her, nudging her bottom insistently. She rubbed against the taut cords of muscle lining his stomach, pressing her damp, needy flesh against him. He growled in warning.

Their eyes met and she froze. Along with the same devastatingly volatile reaction that they'd brought out in each other from the beginning, she saw something more in his expression. And that something made her heart pound in ferocious hope against her breast, as if fighting to be free.

Damon seemed more lighthearted, more at ease with himself than he'd been since the moment they'd met. Maybe it was their recent sexual marathon. Maybe it was the sharing of his painful past. Whatever the reason, it made her pulse leap for joy to see it.

He looked at her through eyes filled with tender emotion. She wasn't anywhere near brave enough to call it love. But it was infinitely promising.

Whatever he felt, she knew Danu was right. Damon was her match, her mate. She would never love another.

She leaned down from her position on top to kiss him, slow and tender. She conveyed through her lips her absolute adoration and devotion. She pulled back to see his expression of wonder, smiling softly into his eyes as she lifted her hips, braced herself above him, slowly sliding down his length.

Their shouts met and merged as their bodies joined. In this position, she could feel him going further than he'd ever been. She wasn't even sure if she could fit all of him inside her slightly sore and swollen sex.

Damon held her hips in his squeezing grasp, trying not to pump himself up into her, to give her time to stretch around him. The honeyed heat of her pussy was scalding his cock, her panting cries killing him. He wanted to roll her over and pound her into the bed beneath him, the need to take over almost strangling him.

He satisfied himself with focusing on retracting two claws, amazed he had that much control as he reached between their bodies to rub her clit between his fingers. He placed just enough pressure to pull a sexy whimper from between her lips, a new gush of fluid from her core easing her way as she slid a few more inches down.

Damon took a groaning breath. *Oh gods, she was so fucking tight.*

Let her take the lead. He could do this for her. He wanted to do this for her. She deserved at least this much after the way he manhandled her in the library, taking her virginity.

And last night. He couldn't seem to keep his hands off her, to stop fucking her, even though he knew she must be sore. But she never once complained, never denied him. In fact, more than once he'd woken to feel her hands exploring him, her tempting mouth on his skin.

He'd never known anyone like Meru. This petite, innocent human was wilder than any oversexed Fae in the realm. She met him need for need.

If not for his abilities, he would never have believed he'd been the first. That such an innocent would so easily rip away his control. Knowing that he'd been the only one…he had to stop this train of thought. He would keep the reins on his wolf if it killed him.

Meru threw her head back as she raised her hips up, rising until only the very tip of his cock remained inside her. She took a deep lungful of air before sliding slowly home, not stopping until her dewy curls were tangled in the thatch of hair around his shaft, until he was all the way in.

"*Mine.*" She whispered at the painfully pleasurable feeling that spread throughout her body. So deep, so full.

She heard him cry out as he registered the soft, adamant declaration. Taking control even from beneath her as he held her hips and rammed his own upward furiously.

Spirals of color and light, the energy she'd gotten used to over the past several days, suddenly burst before her eyes in all its deep, brilliant glory. He seemed to grow even thicker within her, stretching her impossibly wide as he pressed deep and hard and to her soul.

Her orgasm came swiftly, shaking through her body like a storm, her inner muscles rippling around him in rapturous bliss.

He slid from the bed, still inside her as he carried her on strong, determined legs to the bathroom.

"Damon, what are you—"

A low, continuous growl rumbled against her breasts and she gasped in surprise, holding on for the ride. Each strong flex of his thighs pressed their hips together, thrust his cock deeper inside her.

Moaning open mouthed against his shoulder, she licked the salt off his glistening skin, feeling the urgency rising within her once more.

She wrapped her quivering arms around his neck as he leaned over to adjust the temperature, stepping beneath the waterfall style spigot above their heads, drenching them both.

The water was warm, but still she gasped as it pounded against her highly sensitized flesh. Damon hadn't said a word, just dove into her open mouth and fed on her. Voracious.

She tasted her desire on his tongue again, mingled with the dark spice of him that she'd grown to crave. The coppery flavor of her blood as his fangs nicked her lips, but she merely hummed appreciatively, glorying in his wild response.

He pressed her against the tiled wall. She wrapped her legs around him, holding on tightly as he slammed his cock deep again and again. His continuous growl purred from his lips to hers and his grip on her tightened further, clutching her closer as if she would escape his pounding thrusts.

She felt herself coming again, distantly wondering if she'd actually ever stopped, when he suddenly pulled back, looking hungrily at her throat, the muscles in his face roiling, skin growing tighter with the need to change. She must have made a small noise at the sight, because his blistering gaze jerked toward hers before looking away guiltily.

He stilled his body for a single, charged moment, the water roaring over them, drowning out their gasping breaths, the pounding of their hearts.

He roared her name and thrust hard against her once…twice more, his powerful release sending shock waves through her still pulsing pussy. His hips continued to pump against her for long minutes, emptying himself inside her.

Every time. It got better every time, she marveled. It seemed impossible to her. And yet, it was nothing less than the truth. Was it because she loved him? Or did the old adage "practice makes perfect" apply even in this intimate situation?

She was still lost in her inner musings as Damon released her to slide down his body, stepping back and turning away to lean his forehead against the wall.

"Damon?" She reached out a hand to touch his broad, muscled back and he flinched. Unable to stem the hurt his action had caused, she leaned on the other side of the white marbled tile, crossing her arms over her breasts defensively as the steam wafted around them.

"I lost it." His voice sounded so gruffly defeated. Her heart melted a little in sympathy — but she knew that this was too important an issue to ignore in favor of coddling.

"Yeah. It was awesome." Her matter-of-fact tone of voice had him whipping around in shocked anger.

"Awesome?" He looked her over from head to toe. His sharp eyes honed in instantly on the new bruises already forming on her pale hips.

To match the ones she'd received from her ex, he berated himself snidely. He saw the full lower lip his kisses had bloodied, the man shouting an agonized denial even as the wolf howled in hungry triumph.

"There is nothing *awesome* about what I did to you, Meru. What I almost did." He stepped forward, unable to help himself as he placed his finger gently against her swollen lip.

"I bruised you, cut you. Hell, I practically raped you when you were already sore because of my inability to control myself."

When she didn't look impressed, he added harshly, "Baby, I almost completely *changed*! I almost bit you. Wanted to sink my teeth into your throat and taste your blood more than I wanted to *breathe*."

Meru did look a little startled at that. Startled...and slightly intrigued.

He groaned in frustration. What was the matter with the woman, anyway? Didn't she have a single ounce of self-preservation? She should be running screaming from the room, not looking at him like he was an overdramatic child throwing a pointless tantrum.

"When was the last time you did? Completely change, I mean." She was looking at him oddly, studying him with those piercing blue eyes as she waited for his answer.

"Not since Myrddin taught me to control my abilities."

"Not since Myr—three *thousand* years? You haven't fully changed in three millennia? How is that possible? What about all the battles Val was telling Sheridan about yesterday?"

He shrugged. "I've learned how to take what I need from the wolf. Strength, heightened senses, weapons..." He raised his hands bitterly. "I don't need to give myself up to the beast to defeat the *Dark*. I control *it*. It doesn't control me."

His laugh was grim. "Until I met you. Since I caught your scent, I've been a hairsbreadth from changing practically every five minutes."

She rolled her eyes and clucked her tongue disappointedly. "Poor wolf."

"What?" Nothing she'd said could have surprised him more.

"Poor wolf," she repeated easily. "I feel sorry for him. Never gets to play. Never gets to fight. He must feel like he's in Lycan purgatory."

The wolf inside him rolled over and whined pitifully in agreement. Damon ignored him. He couldn't believe Meru didn't understand. Not after all he'd told her last night. She must have read his expression.

"Have you ever come across any other Lycans since that night?" she asked softly.

"A few of Theron's goons early on but none in a very long time. I've been told that most destroyed themselves within the first several hundred years. Many of the men were so overwhelmed, they couldn't change back and ended up dying. Either from grief or by allowing themselves to be caught by the hunters."

She nodded as if she expected as much. "It must have been a shock to them all when they'd seen what they had done the next day. But why would a Lycan, in the full throes of 'wolfiness', be conscious enough to even be capable of remorse? Why would an animal bent on self preservation allow its weak, human predators to slaughter it without a fight?"

He looked down at her waterlogged features, stunned.

He had never wondered. Had never for a moment considered it from that point of view. The few that had run him down had been just as untamed, just as ferocious and grotesquely rabid as his memories of that long ago night. Then again, he recalled, the men loyal to Theron had always been a murderous, bloodthirsty lot.

He understood what she was trying to imply. Hawk had been trying to tell him the same thing the other night. That, as a Lycan, the creature inside him was just an extension of who he was, not a separate entity. That being the case, it stood to reason that if he was not a rapist or a murderer, then the wolf was also innocent of those crimes.

Inside him, the voice that he'd always ignored argued the point, showing him images of the gentle way the beast had carried his dying mother to safety. Of the look of horror and loss in King Lycaon's demonic eyes as he'd begged for his own death.

It was still a new thing, this idea rattling around in his head. That he might not be a monster. His mother's torn body was a visual tattooed on his brain, his warning to himself, his safety. But he was remembering a bit more clearly now.

The king had never had control of his passions where Damon's mother was concerned. And Damon, the mortal man, had always secretly wanted to rescue her, wanted to hurt his sire for causing her pain. The hot, instinctual emotions of the Lycan had only aggravated a situation that already existed.

He was still upset that he had hurt Meru, even remotely, even in passion. He would just have to be more careful, he thought resolutely as he realized he had taken her in his arms and was caressing her back almost absently.

It had taken him only a few years of practice to control the change when it had first happened. Surely with all this time under his belt, all this experience, he could learn in no time to keep his head, regardless of how provocative or sexually impulsive she proved to be, with just a little bit more patience.

Meru had been looking at him. Watching as his thoughts flowed clearly over his expressive face. He is so very beautiful, so perfectly masculine, she thought to herself on a sigh.

And so incredibly stubborn. And obtuse.

It was obvious that he had reaffirmed his desire to hold on to his precious control, regardless of the revelations he'd appeared to be having only seconds earlier.

Nudging his chin toward her, caressing his rough, stubbly cheek with her fingers, she caught his gaze.

"Sometimes," she stated quietly, "you remind me of the myth of Sisyphus" His look said he knew the old Greek yarn.

"Always pushing that giant stone up the hill, only to start all over again when you reach the top. The only difference is…no one is punishing you but you. And no one deserves to be punished less."

Damon's expression gentled at her comment and he held her tighter. "Kyle told me you were a sucker for myths and relics." He laughed softly into her wet hair, ignoring the cooling water around him.

"Just so you know. I may be Lycan, but as you can plainly feel," he rubbed his chest against her breasts. "I'm no myth. And I may be old but I am certainly *not* an artifact you can place on a shelf in some museum. What I'm trying to say is, don't make a hero out of me. I'm only flesh and blood."

Meru had gone still halfway through his speech, and when he was done, she found it hard to draw air into her lungs. She knew.

She knew.

"Meru?" Damon leaned back to look in her eyes, his tone worried. She couldn't answer. As if something were blocking her throat. She took one deep breath, then another, before letting out a scream that had him wincing and covering his sensitive ears.

"Damon! I'm sorry but—Holy Hannah!" She leapt up and down, splashing water everywhere. "She said I'd know and I do! Isn't that wonderful?"

He dropped his arms as she victory danced around the large cubicle, his nod placating, his eyes confused. She knew she was grinning like a loon, so excited she felt as if she could jump out of her own skin.

"You're a genius, an absolute genius." She pushed up on her tiptoes and gave him a loud, smacking kiss on the lips. "Oh Damon, I love you!"

They both froze as her words seem to echo off the marvelously acoustic shower walls. Her eyes grew wide in shock as his narrowed and turned predatory. His body bulged and tensed, leaning closer as she leaned further away, stepping out of his arms reach as if poised for flight. She emitted a squeaked, "Oops" before diving out of the shower faster than Damon could pounce.

Her actions had apparently stunned him for a few critical minutes. It was just enough time for her to grab a giant fluffy towel and dive out the bedroom door. She raced to her cousin's room on wings of embarrassment.

Way to go, Meru, she scolded as she threw open her cousin's door, whizzed past Sheridan and locked the latch behind her. She wasn't exactly sure how she thought he would react to her reckless words.

He hadn't seemed disgusted…then again he hadn't fallen to his knees in amorous intent either. He'd just looked at her as if he were, well, hungry. And she, being a predictable little mouse, had run.

Sheridan, wearing a giant football jersey and a scowl, looked at Meru expectantly. After a few moments, when she didn't hear the crazed footsteps of a wet, naked Lycan in the hall, she sighed in relief.

The loopy grin forming once more, she pushed a drenched curl out of her eyes. "I know where to find The Cup of Inspiration."

Chapter Ten

An hour later, Meru was dressed in a pair of comfortable jeans and a pretty blue, capped-sleeve blouse. She was really going to have to do something to thank Fletcher for his early morning arrival at her cousin's door with yet more clothing in her size. The man was eerie; great fashion sense, but eerie.

Sheridan and Lily had been beside themselves with curiosity, prompted no doubt by her sudden arrival in nothing but a towel. But she'd just said she had suddenly realized where to find the artifact and she'd had no thought other than letting them know as soon as possible. It was a lame excuse and they weren't buying it but they let it go.

Fletcher had gathered everyone together in the library while she took a few moments to herself before she had to face Damon again.

Can we say awkward? She'd never told a man she loved him before but she was fairly sure she had screwed up the proper protocol.

Especially that whole fleeing naked from the room part.

She stepped through the doorway and looked around the now crowded room. Lily was sitting on the arm of the big comfy chair nearest the fireplace, chattering happily with a seated Myrddin, Fletcher close at hand.

Kyle was speaking with quiet intensity to Finn and Raj as they stood close together behind the couch. Her gaze quickly skimmed Damon, his burning eyes focused on her as he leaned against the wall, apart from the others.

She tilted her head as she studied Sheridan and Val lost in conversation on the couch. At least, she thought it was Val. The golden energy that she had always seen around him had altered, darkened somehow. His expression as well. The easygoing peacemaker of the *Fianna* seemed to have been replaced by someone quite a bit edgier. Harder. And then there were his eyes.

"You look different." She hadn't realized she had spoken aloud until the hum of conversation in the room ceased and all heads turned her way.

Light amber eyes looked piercingly in her direction. They studied her, looking inside, through her. Meru shivered at the dominance and restrained power that had replaced the charming grin on his handsome face.

Sheridan had risen to join her in the doorway, bubbling with discovery. "You were right, Meru, there *are* two of him!" She whispered loudly. Pointing at the deliciously sprawled Norseman on the couch, she continued.

"That's Hawk. Or as I like to call him…Brad Two." Hawk chuckled at the comment, drawing Meru's fascinated gaze to his once more.

Where Val was charming and playful, Hawk looked dangerous. As if he could take on a bloody battle with single-minded enjoyment and revelry, win it without remorse or compunction, then find a woman and sweep through her defenses with his sheer sexual will, leaving her thanking him for it afterward.

Damon, she'd noticed in the periphery of her vision, had stalked closer to her, placing himself casually in her line of sight by sitting on the arm of the couch, directly between her and the object of her fascinated study.

Hawk laughed a bit more at that. Rising easily from his seated position, he took Meru's hand in his own.

"Nice to finally meet you, little seer." He kissed her hand. Then sniffed her. Once. Twice. He leaned back to look her over once more with eyes that missed nothing, turning his head abruptly to glare at Damon who was doing a fair amount of glowering himself at their still joined hands.

Confused by the undercurrents and determined to distract the two giants before they got into some kind of testosterone tournament in Myrddin's lovely library, she tugged free from the Viking's grasp, stepping further into the room and clearing her throat.

"I know where to find The Cup of Inspiration." That got everyone's attention, she thought, relieved.

Her blue eyes sparkled as she told her story, beginning with a detailed description of her dreamtime conversation with Danu.

She recounted all that Danu had told her. About the Tuatha, about the gifts she had made them and about her apparent loneliness. She'd barely finished when Finn separated himself from the others to stand before her, a solemn look upon his face.

He entered her mind like a burst of brilliant light. It wasn't painful but it was intimate. She felt his presence waiting at the edge of her consciousness, asking permission to enter. She understood his reasons, he wasn't hiding them from her, though she knew he could.

She allowed her dream of Danu rise to the surface of her thoughts and invited him to share the vision. His awe and reverence was a tangible thing. A supplicant who had never seen the face of his True Queen, never had her voice to guide him.

Meru felt like an intruder in her own mind. Witnessing such a personal moment, though it surprised her, was nothing compared to what he did next. The arrogant, handsome noble kneeled humbly at her feet, looking directly into her eyes as he spoke within her mind.

Forgive me for doubting you, priestess of Danu. As a Fianna, you have always had my protection. As a prince of the House of Aisling, one of the children of Danu, the Tuatha Dé Danaan, I offer you my life.

You and all you love now have the fealty of my people, of me. I make this vow to you in the name of The True Queen.

Meru was overcome and felt tears prick her eyes at the words reverberating in her head. Here was a being of light and Magick. An immortal warrior and an exceedingly proud member of the Fae race.

Though he had a tendency toward swaggering sarcasm and gave every appearance of apathy, Finn was no less powerful or impressive for it.

His tone was formal. Lavender eyes so sincere that she had no doubt that she had just attained something only a few others, most of them in this room, had ever received...the absolute loyalty of this independent warrior.

Silently, unused to this form of communication, she thanked him. Then she pushed a picture of her ornery cousin at him mentally. *Fealty to all I love?* she queried, knowing that Sheridan was difficult as a rule, but particularly standoffish around this particular Tuatha.

She felt a wave of uncomfortably strong emotion. Emotion that Meru was sure Finn hadn't meant her to feel as he responded to the visual she had sent him. Self-mockery swiftly followed as he answered.

Regardless of the difficult task you have laid before me, I believe I am up to the challenge.

"Anytime you two lovebirds are done with this riveting tableau of chivalry, you can join the rest of us in holding back our ticked-off leader."

She jerked her gaze upward to find the rest of the room gazing at them oddly. Hawk, the one who had made the amused comment, stood beside Damon, holding his arm casually. The Lycan's other arm was in the hands of the ever serene Raj. Damon's muscles bulged and his dark eyes flamed at Finn's rising form, a dangerous snarl curling his lip.

Finn, aware of the seriousness of the warning, seemed to communicate silently with Damon for a moment. Whatever he was saying relaxed the Lycan, allowing the men holding him to take a relieved step back.

Sheridan looked a little ticked at the scene as well, sidling close to Meru to say, half jokingly, "Are you making up for lost time or something? No men for three decades and then, boom—a boatload of supermen in a few days?"

She rolled her eyes dismissively at her cousin. If she didn't know better, she'd say Sheridan had been jealous of the attention the auburn-haired Faerie had given to Meru.

Myrddin caught her eye as he sat there watching the scene unfold like a proud papa and Meru took a step closer to him. He noted the concern in her gaze and he took her hand, pulling her closer.

"What is it, my dear girl?"

Meru shuffled a bit before responding. "The last thing Danu said was for you."

His brow rose in interest. "Danu said, 'The answer to your riddle lies in your past. In your weakness for a fickle heart'. Those were her exact words. Do you have any idea what she was talking about?"

It was obvious he did. He rose to his full, impressive height. The silver in his eyes were glowing brilliant as molten steel, the light around his head glimmering dangerously. Lily and Fletcher both took a concerned step back, feeling the menace in his manner.

His face took on a tortured expression as he closed his eyes on one whispered word. "Nimue."

Lily, who knew the love story of Nimue and Merlin as well as anyone, instinctively tensed beside him at the mention of the woman. Myrddin shook his head at her sadly and pulled her to his side.

"Not *every* myth is true, my love." He stated in a low voice almost too soft for Meru to hear. Then he straightened and turned to the others.

"I have to call together The Council. Find the Cup, keep the women safe. I will return as quickly as I can." He kissed Lily passionately, nearly bending her back across his arm, before setting her beside Fletcher with a silent order to protect her before he flashed away.

Damon laid a hand on her shoulder. Meru realized she had been staring at the space where Myrddin had made his abrupt departure for several, silent minutes. She was dying to know what he'd gotten from Danu's words and what it had to do with the legendary Nimue.

"You said you knew the location of the Cup."

"Yes. Actually you gave me the idea in the shower when you—" Meru's face turned purple with embarrassment as she realized what she had just said. Out loud in front of everyone. Various looks of glee and discomfort shuttled around the library, Kyle looking especially flabbergasted.

Damon's expression couldn't have been more satisfied. His grin was dark and sexy, gaze confident and knowing. He couldn't have been more obvious.

"Geesh. Why don't you just beat your chest while you're at it?" Meru muttered, causing Finn to choke on a laugh, looking at the ceiling quickly when Damon turned to glare.

"*Anyway,*" she stressed, still mortified. "It came to me in a flash, a picture of the Cup. I know where it is. It's sitting on a shelf, in the basement of the museum where I interned."

Her college career had been slow going, mostly because the scholarships didn't cover everything and she had had to work, whenever possible, to come up with the funds she needed to live. She had started interning at the museum when she was a sophomore, working there every summer until she'd gotten her Master's.

Even after she'd gotten the assistant teaching position for her favorite professor while she worked on her doctorate, she'd still helped out at the museum every other weekend until she'd left school.

"Are you sure that it's the right one? Isn't that a little strange? Not to mention convenient."

This from Kyle, ever the fact gatherer, caused her to nod adamantly. "Without a doubt. When Danu was describing the artifact's properties to me, how it would be drawn to my location, I got a distinct picture in my mind of what it looked like."

She grew excited as she continued. "And then this morning, I saw it again and this time I remembered where I'd seen it before. The summer the museum director took me under his wing and allowed me to catalogue the entire shipment of Roman artifacts we'd received from this eccentric, old collector."

"Roman?" Raj jumped in, listening with rapt interest.

"Yes. What we discovered in the original dig records, as well as the style and distinctive markings on the objects themselves, caused us to postulate that a large section of the artifacts found at that particular site were probably the booty from Caesar's bloody raid on the Celtic Gauls."

Damon leaned his chin on her shoulder, causing her to stiffen in surprise. A tingling spark of awareness quickly spread through her limbs.

Memories from this morning swamped her. She felt herself grow wet as his lips caressed her ear. His tongue flicked over one tender lobe and then he spoke, too quietly for anyone but her to hear him.

"You're so sexy when you're studious."

Meru shivered. He was incredibly distracting. And what did his behavior mean? Was he pretending her earlier declaration hadn't happened? Or was he trying to tell her that he still wanted her even though he didn't feel the same? Was she overanalyzing? Probably.

She stepped away from his heat and tried to concentrate. "Yes, well, that is…" She stammered a bit, trying to recall what she'd been talking about.

"Those artifacts included one plain earthen cup adorned with what we thought at the time was a simple symbol for water. After learning what I have in the past few days, I believe it is Danu's mark."

She walked to the marble fireplace, her brain buzzing with the possibilities. "For reasons known only to the Cup itself, it must have appeared to them and, honoring the Druid way, they had to have had some idea of its importance. They must have recognized the mark of their goddess.

The Romans hated the Gauls, would have wanted to keep only those mementos, those *things* that the people held dear or sacred. It's a miracle that it wasn't broken or destroyed over the years. It was found in perfect condition nearly two millennia later. Eventually, it found its way to a basement in a Houston museum and to me, where it had meant to go all along."

Everyone silently pondered this information before Finn shrugged and snapped his fingers. "Well, this should be a piece of cake then. I'll pop in, grab the thing and be back before Fletcher gets breakfast on the table."

Meru was already shaking her head. "You can't. Didn't you hear what I told you? Danu created this particular object so that neither you nor anyone like you would be able to touch it. I have no idea what would happen to you if you tried to get it yourself. I'll have to come with you."

"Absolutely not." Damon's stern, rasping voice was unbending. He folded his thick arms and narrowed his eyes, the essence of male pique.

"You can*not* tell me what to do, Damon Arkadios." Meru stuck out her chin, willing to be just as stubborn as she scowled at the irritating man.

"I can. And I will." Damon stated calmly. "I am the leader of the *Fianna*, put in charge of ensuring your protection. And I will do my job, regardless of what you say or think to the contrary."

He looked at Finn, ignoring her indignant gasp. "If we can't touch it, we have to bring a human along to carry the thing. I'm thinking Kyle." Kyle nodded quickly. "We still can't risk using any Magick outside of this house that might draw the *Dark*. They'll be lying in wait to follow our trail and get their hands on Meru."

"Again with the no Magick rule." Finn groaned dramatically. "We can kick their scaly tails if they follow us, but no, let's go with the plan that will take all bloody day!"

Damon ignored him. He knew Finn would never question or refuse his leadership. They had been through too much together.

The others, however, were another matter entirely. They had moved to form a united front beside Meru.

Sheridan, Lily and a protective looking Fletcher closed ranks around her. She was giving him a look that could mean anything. Anything except that she'd do exactly as he said without complaint.

"If you're not using Magick, you won't be able to get *in* there without me." Her arms crossed defensively under her breasts, framing them in what Damon thought was an effectively distracting way.

"Huh?" He grunted, his eyes unable to leave those incredibly full mounds he'd been suckling just a few hours before.

"She's right." Kyle drew his gaze, not helping Damon's stance at all with his comment. "That museum she's talking about? I know the company they hired to do their security. They are loaded for bear in there. All the latest detection devices, video surveillance, even those top-notch sensor panels on the floor. There's no way you'd just be able to walk in undetected."

"Unless the museum director thought you were cute, you had a key to the employee entrance *and* knew the code to use on the keypad to disable the security alarms." Sheridan indicated Meru with a tilt of her head, causing the men in the room to look at the smaller woman with grudging respect.

"He doesn't think I'm cute." She huffed to her cousin under her breath. Sheridan snorted.

"Sure. That's why—" Meru whipped around, glaring warningly until her cousin subsided.

"Now is not the time." She looked back at Damon, her stance challenging.

Damon was quiet for a moment, weighing what they'd told him. He knew there was no way she was going to give him the access code or the key. Just as he knew she was not going to back down about joining this little raiding party.

He could probably have Finn pull it from her mind but everything in him rejected that option. Not only did the idea of the intimate connection that would create between his woman and the playboy Tuatha make his blood boil, he was also pretty sure she wouldn't thank him for the intrusion.

More than anything else in the world, he wanted to keep Meru safe from the *Dark*. What he should do is leave her chained to her bed so he'd know where she was at all times.

He thought of her spread out on that silken cover, her arms stretched out toward the large posts of her bedframe. She'd be naked, her body laid out before him like a feast. His mouth watered at the thought of all he could do to her. How many ways he could—

"Hey, Wolfie." Sheridan was clapping her hands loudly in front of his face to get his attention. "Not to interrupt your obviously personal daydream..."

She *hadn't* just looked at the bulge forming in the front of his pants, he told himself bracingly. "But we have a situation we need to resolve. Are you going to say we can come? Or are we going to have to follow behind you and finish the job while you get arrested?"

Damon looked at his men, who both shrugged in agreement, before stalking over to stand directly in front of the tiny woman who held his heart. He watched her eyes go soft as she took in his expression. He took her in his arms, heedless of the others.

"Fine. You can go. See? I'm not a completely unreasonable man." He smiled down at her for a moment before he tightened his grip on her back.

"Now it's your turn. When we're there, you do everything I say, no questions asked. Knowing," he continued as Sheridan began to raise her voice in protest. "that I only have your safety, everyone's safety, in mind."

Meru looked up at the man she loved. He was wrong about himself. He was every inch a hero.

Her first eyeful of this dark mountain of a man had made her think of a Greek god, but he was so much more honorable, so much braver, than any god she'd ever read about. And he cared about her. She knew he did.

Beyond the task he'd been given by Myrddin to watch over her, beyond his general duties as a portal guardian, he really cared about *her*.

Knowing that, it was the easiest thing in the world to smile and say, "Of course, Damon."

* * * * *

Hawk was angry. From the expression on Dragon Boy's face, he could tell that Raj was disturbed as well. They had cornered Damon after the women went to the kitchen with Fletcher, planning to get some kind of meal together for lunch since they'd skipped breakfast.

They took him to the workout room to spar. Hawk thought this was the best room in the old Archon's house. Wall-to-wall weaponry of every imaginable kind from more eras than he was familiar with.

Weight machines and stationary bicycles just wouldn't cut it for Myrddin's group of supernaturals. No, they got their workouts by pummeling each other in the giant, padded ring that took up most of the ballroom-sized arena.

The wolf, the hawk and the dragon all circled the ring as they sized each other up.

Damon, though he usually didn't use any weaponry apart from his Lycan abilities, carried a Scottish claymore easily in one of his massive hands. The blade was nearly four feet in length, but nowhere near as wide and intimidating as Hawk's sword, which was a close replica to his own.

Raj's tall, lean body flowed around the ring like water. He wove two short bahi sticks around in his hands. The Bahi were thick, hardwood sticks used in the Filipino fighting style *eskrima*. In the knowledgeable hands of Raj, they could be more effective than either of the swords combined.

"You have a serious problem, Arkadios," Hawk began aggressively, stalking his friend with his sword held snugly in both hands. The ringing tone of clanging swords filled the room as the sparring began.

Raj and Hawk seemed to join forces, surrounding the confident Damon, who easily dodged and deflected both the Viking sword and the hypnotic Bahi sticks.

In a feat that would have been impossible for an ordinary man, Damon used his Lycan agility to leap high, rolling in midair to land behind his two opponents, escaping the corner they had crowded him into.

"And I'm sure you're going to tell me just what that problem is," Damon said smiling, slicing the Claymore easily through the empty air.

"You haven't mated our little seer yet." Hawk ducked out of the way smoothly as Damon whirled on him in surprise. Their swords clashed, both men's superior strength causing the metal to vibrate with unnatural intensity.

"We all know you've been with her." Another swing sent Hawk soaring above Damon's lowered arm, landing directly behind him to whack the broad hilt of his Viking blade against his back in warning. "But you've yet to make it official, as it were."

Raj, circling his arms in a whirlwind of elegant motion, got several body shots in even as he parried Damon's attempts to skewer him.

Not even breathing heavily after several minutes of the rough play, he spoke with quiet composure. "What Hawk is trying to say is you haven't bitten her." The shock on Damon's face mirrored itself in his fists as his grip on the Scottish sword momentarily went lax.

It was all the opening Raj needed to wrap his sticks around the blade, twirling it loose from Damon's hands and sending it sailing through the air.

Raj's body copied the motion, spinning into a low kick meant to lay Damon out on the mat. Though distracted, Damon's instincts were too deeply ingrained. Falling into a backflip to land crouched between his would-be attackers, he grasped two sets of ankles with his newly emerged claws and brought the men tumbling down beside him.

Hawk knew the fact that Raj had been able to disarm Damon, even momentarily, showed that their leader was obviously out of sorts and in shock. A Damon not distracted by his feelings for Meru was unbeatable. That was one of the reasons he knew it was so imperative to resolve this situation as quickly as possible.

They laid down their weapons and sat up beside Damon in the middle of the fighting ring.

Raj wrapped his arms around his raised knees and stared at the far wall. "I am dragonkind of Shambhala, and similar to the way of the Therians, the shifter species, I must mark my mate when I find her to seal her fate to mine."

Hawk whacked Damon on his shoulder as he sat quietly between them. "And don't start flapping your fangs with that 'I'm not a real shifter, I'm cursed' nonsense. According to DB here, most of the natural shifter rules apply to you as well."

Damon sat up, running his hands through his hair as he tried to unclench his jaw. "Not that it's any of your fucking business," he grated, "but you're right. I haven't bitten her. It's taken all my control not to—but I haven't. And honestly, I don't plan on that changing anytime soon."

Raj turned his head, leaning it on his knee as he looked into angry black eyes. "You think you would lose yourself to the wolf when, in fact, the wolf would rather die than hurt her. You think it would kill her when, in fact, it would protect her from harm."

Damon glowered at the Shambhalan, who sat there so calmly as he tempted Damon's strongest desire, his deepest fear. "Thank you, oh wise guru of the mountaintop. What exactly do you mean by that convoluted statement?"

"He means that when a shifter bites his mate, not only does he ensure the ability of procreation, but he also gives her a little bit of his essence. They can communicate telepathically, sense each other's emotions. Find each other no matter where they are. This helps the shifter to protect his mate, to keep her safe." Hawk looked at Damon pointedly as he spoke, watching the realization sink in.

Damon had known all this from his past observations of Therians but had never applied it to his own situation. The last few days had been full of one revelation after another. Had he been so wrapped up in self-loathing and pity that he hadn't been able to see the truth that had stared him in the face for so long?

He thought about his desire to bite Meru. It was a powerful need, similar to an addict's need for a fix. But it wasn't a violent hunger. No. It was entirely sexual. Possessive and passionate.

Mate. She was his mate. The thought of joining so completely with her that he would be able to share her thoughts and feeling was indescribable.

"Ah, light dawns." Emerald eyes smiled, softening the sarcasm. "You've done well, grasshopper." The men laughed as they all slowly got to their feet.

"There's another plus side to fully mating Meru." Hawk offered his hand to tug Damon up off the mat. "You'd finally relax enough to stop growling every time one of us got within ten feet of her."

"Don't bet on it." Damon shook his head as he thought about his volatile reaction to the curly-haired pixie in the other room. "Now I just have to tell her that she's my mate and, in order for us to live happily forever after, she has to trust me enough not to kill her while I'm gnawing on her flesh. Yeah, I bet she'll love that."

"Don't underestimate Meru, Damon. She's a lot stronger than even she knows yet. And she loves you. When you both want to see something eerie, have her show you the part of the prophecy Áine wrote for her. Trust me. It's an interesting read. When you understand what it means." And with that cryptic remark, Raj led the way out of the sparring room, each of them heading in different directions.

As much as Damon wanted to, he couldn't get Meru alone for the rest of the day. She was caught up in discussions with the others or helping in the kitchen with Fletcher, who seemed to be a little smitten with her himself.

He might have taken offense to her obvious avoidance tactics but his mind was distracted. His head full of images of them together, of a future that he hadn't even dared to consider before.

He felt energized, nearly reborn. No longer was the cloud of the curse hovering over his head. Just like any other shifter, he could love his mate and keep her safe. He could give her children. Little girls with big blue eyes and freckles like their mother. He could have a family.

When it was time to head toward the now closed museum, Damon kept close to the effervescent Meru. She seemed so excited. As if they were going on an adventure. And her smile was contagious. He couldn't wait to get her back to her bedroom. To show her how very special she had become to him. Tell her how he felt.

Their little gathering of would-be crooks grew smaller throughout the day. Kyle had called to check in at the precinct, only to be informed of an emergency powwow with the police chief. The subject, of course, was the whereabouts of the missing women.

Fletcher informed them as they walked out the door that he and Lily would be staying behind. He was taking his order to protect Myrddin's paramour very seriously. Fortunately, Lily had no problems being left out of "The Heist" as she laughingly called it. Raj also declined, saying he had some research he wanted to take care of.

The added muscle was in no way missed. It was, in fact, the simplest break-in in recorded history. So easy it made Damon nervous.

Meru waved at Jim, the regular security guard, who obviously still remembered her. Damon had to curl his nails hard into his palms to keep from reacting to the short man who blushed bashfully at the sight of *his* mate. She used her key to open the door, quickly punching in the seven-digit code that turned off the security system.

When the five of them entered the climate controlled basement, he saw Finn and Val's jaws drop. He had to admit it was hard not to be impressed at the museum's collection.

Rows of shelves filled with treasures from every age, busts and small statuary, mysterious boxes labeled with coding, Egyptian sarcophagi. And that was just down the first row.

Meru, having seen it all many times before, headed straight for the clipboard against the wall. "All these codes have been entered into the museum computer's database, but the director doesn't really trust the technology, so he makes sure a paper copy is always available.

Sifting through the lists, she headed down one of the aisles, Damon on her heels. The others wandered around, the men seeming entranced by the leftover riches of the past they themselves had lived through.

Meru had her nose buried in her clipboard and would have run into an opened box left on the floor if he hadn't steered her around it. She turned the corner and went directly to a large, sealed plastic container on the closest shelf. Opening it quickly, she smiled and looked over her shoulder at Damon. "Jackpot."

Her gamine grin was so adorable, the exhilaration in her eyes too much to resist as Damon pressed her against the cluttered shelf, his erection rubbing against her jean-clad behind while he took her mouth with hungry intent.

She gasped and he swallowed the sound, taking advantage of her parted lips, his tongue thrusting deep, filling her mouth as he wanted to fill her body.

He felt her body relax against his, lost to reason as he slid his hands beneath her top to touch the silken curve of her belly. It wasn't the time or the place but he couldn't seem to help himself.

He unsnapped her jeans with more aggression than finesse, the button clattering unnoticed to the floor.

"You're already wet for me." He lifted his lips from hers, his gravelly voice a harsh whisper of sound against her ear. He could smell her. Reveled in the sweetness of it, remembering how she tasted on his tongue, how she felt around him.

Slipping his hand over the soft, soft skin of her belly, he waited for her breath to catch and her beautiful blue eyes to meet his as they locked together in this silent moment of irresistible need. He rubbed his palm over her clit, her hips pressing back against his at the intense sensation. Damon growled low as he pressed two thick fingers deep inside her, stretching her tight sheath as she drenched his hand.

"I need inside, Meru. I want to feel this tight cunt wrapped around my cock. I want to fuck you until neither one of us can move. As soon as this is over..." He left the sentence hanging as a loud moan bubbled up from her throat. He ate at her lips, his erection pressing painfully against its denim prison.

He could feel how close she was already, how attuned to his touch. Her hips frantically fucked his fingers as she held on to the shelving above her head, kissing him back with desperate passion.

His fingers still pumping deep and fast, Damon pressed the rough pad of his thumb against her swollen clit. Meru stiffened in his arms, a stifled scream lodged in her throat as she came on his hand, the heady aroma of her arousal making Damon curse this impromptu session.

He would throw her down on the cold floor and take her now but he'd seen Finn grab an open-mouthed Sheridan and pull her out of sight only moments before.

Thankful for his friend's quick thinking, and more than a little embarrassed by his own lapse of good judgment, Damon stepped away from his recovering mate. Brushing a damp curl from her forehead, he kissed her tenderly, smiling into her dazed expression.

"I think we should grab the Cup and leave as quickly as possible." He heard her snort in disbelief, glaring at him as she straightened her clothes and passed a shaky hand over her face. After a moment, she nodded and reached to open the container.

He saw her unwrap and lift the innocuous-looking clay goblet, of a style he'd seen a million times in the past. Not jeweled or golden, it looked like a simple peasant's cup.

She turned fully around, holding her prize tightly in her hands as she glanced up at him. Her expression turned to one of horror just as he caught the scent. Her pale face looking over his shoulder was the last thing he saw as he felt a sharp, stabbing sensation in his neck. He was instantly paralyzed. And then the world went dark.

Meru was horrified. She opened her mouth to scream when she felt a clammy hand, rippling with scales, cover her face. She too was stabbed in the neck, probably with the same type of syringe she'd seen that snarling wolf-man ram into Damon. And before she could utter a single protest, she sagged into the arms of her sneering captor. They vanished quietly. Without a trace.

Chapter Eleven

෨

"Wake up, darling."

Meru felt the ice cold tickle of a damp, pointed tongue against her cheek and tried not to flinch. She thought perhaps if she pretended she was still knocked out, the *Sauros*, who could be no other than Allen Thorne, would go away and let her get her bearings.

She was upright but bound by her wrists and ankles to a smooth wall. From the way Thorne's voice echoed, she imagined the room she was in must be cavernous, but she was too afraid to open her eyes to find out.

Damon. What had become of him? Was he here with her, bound as she was, but still unconscious? She couldn't believe it had happened so quickly. She could only pray to Danu that he was still alive and try like hell to get out of here. Wherever *here* was.

"I know you're awake, Meru. Don't be a coward." His voice harsher now that he hadn't immediately gotten his way, Thorne slapped her across the face.

Her eyes came open with a snap as she turned her head toward him, the angry handprint on her cheek no match for the ire in her eyes.

"Let me out of these cuffs, Allen. Then we'll see who the coward is." Thorne laughed in delight and clapped his hands mockingly.

"So brave." He sneered condescendingly. "Or do you think someone will save you before I take you at your word?"

She turned away from him without answering to study her prison. It was a giant bedroom of some sort, but it looked strange, as if the rules of gravity didn't apply.

Pictures moved, chairs floated and even the bed seemed to alter its shape and size as she watched. And Damon was nowhere to be found.

The décor, an odd mixture of gaudy depravity and overindulgence, nearly made her queasy. Garish blood red fabric draped everything and oddly shaped mirrors hung on every available wall, giving the room the dizzying disturbed feel of a fun house at a carnival.

"Is this where you live? No wonder you never invited me over. Did you decorate in early narcissist or late seventies gigolo? I must say it's very you." She knew she shouldn't antagonize him, that she should be lulling him into a false sense of security and finding out where they'd taken Damon. But she couldn't seem to stop the angry vitriol that was coming out of her mouth. Her family put in danger, The Willow's Knot destroyed, their future uncertain…it was enough to make her snap.

Thorne's creepy eyes narrowed, his scales seeming to stand on end in annoyance.

"I'd expected weeping and pleading. Three months I spent with a pathetic chit who showed no fire, no spark. The closest you came to passion was when you were discussing your beloved theories."

He gripped her chin, forcing her to face him. "I feel a little cheated, my love. Robbed somehow for the time I had to spend wooing you, placating you, with nothing to show for it. And now I can sense that Lycan on you. Months of effort and you let that hot-blooded, uncivilized mutt rut on you like a bitch in heat. That doesn't exactly endear you to me, so you should be careful what you say, darling. Your fate is, after all, in my hands."

She laughed harshly. "Better a wolf than a cold-blooded reptile. You were a smooth operator, Allen, but a lousy boyfriend, a terrible kisser and a bad student. I'm actually relieved it was all an act. There is simply no way that *you're* the mastermind behind this little coup."

Thorne had raised his hand to strike her once more, looking angrier than she could recall seeing him, when a voice off to the side made him pause.

"I told you that you could play with her later, Thorny." The soft, sweet, singsong voice sent a chill through her trapped limbs. She strained her neck to look around Allen, seeking out the owner. What she saw confounded her.

The most beautiful woman she had ever set eyes on, apart from Danu, walked slowly toward her. Her body was grace in motion. Willowy and slender as a reed, she glided and swayed toward Meru as if she were underwater, every movement entrancing.

Her skin was the same shimmering olive as Damon's, as Myrddin's. Her hair dangled down her back in a thousand tiny, ebony braids, each one twined with thin strands of gold.

And around her head, the same nimbus of light that crowned Myrddin's like a halo. *Must be an Archon thing*, Meru decided with a nervous shiver.

The woman's dress was Grecian-style, the material the same blood-red velvet that covered the room. It was her face, however, that really drew and held Meru's attention.

It was the face of an innocent goddess, of an entrancing, sensual, utterly fragile female. The personification of forbidden temptation. Only her wide, slanted eyes, clouded silver and glowing with psychotic excitement, kept Meru's guard up against her.

Thorne bowed toward the woman, sliding one last, leering grin toward Meru as he went to stand by the curtain that hid the entranceway.

As the woman stood before her, Meru felt her wolf's torc warm around her neck. She'd almost forgotten it was there. A sudden, familiar breeze that smelled of spring and sweet lavender surrounded her for a heartbeat…and she knew.

"You're Nimue."

Nimue frowned petulantly. "And you're too smart for your own good." She glanced toward Thorne before smirking over to where Meru hung from the wall.

"Well, except in matters of the heart. First you fell for my sneaky little *Sauros* and then you give yourself to that cursed *Fianna*, that devil's spawn of Lycaon." Her eyes softened as if lost in thought. "But then, we women are always victims of our tender hearts."

Meru tried to stop her voice from shaking as she asked the question that had been screaming through her mind since she'd regained consciousness. "Where is Damon?"

Nimue giggled and clapped her hands together like a little child. "Oh Thorny, look how she trembles! The worry and terror in her voice when she mentions his name. She must really love him. Unrequited love." She sighed. "How incredibly sad."

She flinched and Nimue saw the sign of weakness, thrusting the dagger in. "You didn't *really* think he loved you, did you? A Lycan *mates* with the woman he loves, bites her and shares himself completely. It's obvious he slept with you. But it would take a lot more woman than we both know you are to satisfy a powerful being like that."

Meru tried to ignore her words, but insecurity rose to the surface. Damon *had* held himself back from biting her on several occasions. She thought it was because he didn't want to hurt her but, what if there was another reason?

What if he simply didn't want to be stuck with her as his mate? Just because she was in love with him didn't mean he returned her feelings. Unfortunately, that possibility didn't lessen them either.

"What have you done with him?" Her voice was firm, despite the heart that felt like it was breaking inside her.

Nimue placed a slender palm to her chest in innocence. "*I* haven't done anything to him. I was a little disturbed when my," she glared pointedly at Thorne, "servants couldn't get him away from you." She shrugged, smiling as she continued. "Luckily, I had already seen that problem coming and made an alliance that I knew would benefit my plans."

"What alliance?"

Nimue spun before one of the wall-to-wall mirrors, watching her dress swirl around her legs, her braids fly through the air as she danced. "The smartest one yet. It would be very hard, even for me, to get that particular goody-two-shoes out of the way. He's too well connected. So I simply asked myself how one would go about killing a Lycan. And the answer appeared as if someone had whispered in my ear."

She turned toward the white-faced Meru and grinned in mischievous insanity.

"If you want to kill one Lycan...you simply need another one. Or two.

* * * * *

Damon was in agony. His blood was burning like acid beneath his flesh from whatever they'd injected him with. Body racked with unimaginable pain. He was on his knees on a floor of hard, damp concrete. A heavy metal slab across his shoulders, his wrists chained tightly to the ends.

He couldn't move. The chains must have been forged from Hephaestus silver, an Archon metal. Myrddin had once told him that it was the only thing in any dimension that could hold a Lycan.

His sense of smell, however, was still working fine. He knew Theron and Kyros were nearby, gloating quietly in the shadows of what looked like an old warehouse.

He had no idea where he was, how they'd gotten a hold of these chains or the transport devices. His only conclusion was that they had been procured from the same mysterious source that had aided the *Sauros*. And the transport devices explained how he hadn't caught their scent at the museum until they were upon him. But what had they given him?

He inwardly railed at himself. How could he have been caught so off guard? And what of Meru? What had happened to his mate? Had the other *Fianna* taken her to safety? Was she even now returned to Myrddin's fortress of a house, wondering where he was? He prayed with all that he was that that was the case. He needed to get back to her to see for himself that she was safe. It was time to end this.

"Honorable as ever, my brothers? Still needing the help of others to best the bastard slave, I see."

He heard the roar of rage before he saw Theron, partially changed and barreling toward him. Kyros dragged behind as he attempted to hold him back.

"Patience, brother! We'll get no satisfaction from granting him such an easy death." The words of Kyros seemed to calm the furious Theron, stopping his clawed hand before he could strike.

His fangs retracting as he continued to stare, unblinking, at Damon, Theron grimaced. "I suppose you're right, Kyros. Though I find myself eager to bathe in the blood of this murderer, vengeance will be all the sweeter for his suffering."

His face an unreadable mask, Damon looked upon the duo that had made the years of his youth so hellish. Time had not been kind to them.

Regardless of the Lycan healing abilities and infinite lifespan, their faces were haggard and gaunt, their bodies riddled with scars. For a Lycan, those could only have been caused by Archon Magick. What had those two gotten themselves into?

How had they survived all these years? It was obvious that they hadn't changed much, despite appearances. Their expressions were still too smugly superior, their eyes still as drenched in malice. It was a miracle someone hadn't killed them long ago.

"Whose panting lapdog have you become, Theron, to have gotten your hands on Hephaestus silver?" Damon wanted to rile him, wanted to force his hand. He wanted to distract his half brother while he rid himself of his shackles.

He owed Myrddin yet another debt, he smiled inwardly, recalling that when the old man had told him of his only weakness, he'd also showed him how to overcome it. He would bet his brothers knew nothing of any Magicks beyond their Lycan abilities. He would use their ignorance to his advantage.

Though Theron tensed, his voice was still calm as he responded. "We have friends just as powerful as yours, little bastard. *More* powerful. And we all agree on one thing. Every one of us wants to see you dead. You and your little whore."

Damon growled, unable to help himself, and Theron knew he'd hit his mark. "That *Sauros* Thorne mentioned something about a little payback before he flashed in to grab her. Something about her not being able to hold out for long, isn't that right, Kyros?"

Kyros chuckled, "That's what he said, brother."

Two shocked cries resounded through the dank prison as Damon, free of his chains and enraged, threw the large metal bar toward them as he rose to tower angrily above them.

The pain in his body pushed aside, Damon's anger gave him strength as he allowed his Lycan gifts to come to the fore. His body expanded, ripping through his grime-covered clothing. Thick claws burst forth from his hands, gleaming sharply in the dim light.

He smiled through the sting of his fangs bursting past his gums as he stalked closer to his cowering brothers. Kyros looked at him, his eyes crazed with fear as he shouted, "You killed our father! Our King! You don't deserve to live, don't deserve to be Lycan!"

Damon suddenly felt a little sorry for the pathetic man. "He killed my mother. An innocent babe. Thousands of men, women and children in his pointless quest for power. But you're right, none of us deserved to be cursed. No one deserved to be punished but our father, the King."

A growling snarl behind him was all the warning he got before he rolled, diving out of the way as Theron took a swipe at his head, claws extended. He'd somehow snuck around him and fully changed while Damon was distracted by Kyros.

He backed up, circling warily as he watched Kyros morph to match his brother, two fully shifted Lycans attempting to trap him between. They were an image out of his long faded nightmares, the beasts he had run so long and far from, as he had from the one within himself.

Covered in a fur lighter than his own, matted and unhealthy, they still looked deadly. Their faces had formed into elongated muzzles, eyes inhumanly bright. They stood on two legs, giant drooling beasts still easily recognizable to Damon.

Theron dove for him, his full Lycan strength sending Damon crashing to the floor beneath him. He flipped Theron over onto his back and hopped up before leaning into a strong legged back kick, knocking the charging Kyros in the jaw with a well placed boot.

Kyros released an animal scream, catching Damon's thigh with his dirt-encrusted claws while falling backward from the blow. Theron, scenting the blood in the air, jumped up and ran once more toward a whirling Damon.

They circled around him, fangs bared, dagger-tipped paws extended toward him warily. Damon allowed them closer, smiling with dark intent. "I haven't got time to play this childhood game with you, Theron. Tell me where they've taken my mate."

Theron spoke in the garbled, rumbling tone of the full Lycan, his sneer apparent even around the fangs. "Somewhere you'll never find her, you bastard son of a slave whore. Somewhere to die."

Sensing Kyros behind him, he allowed himself to be nearly sandwiched between the two brothers before he spoke again. "You're a weakling and a coward, Theron. You don't have the strength to kill me as you think I deserve. To kill me as I killed our father. As I'd kill him again."

Just as Damon knew he would, Theron responded with a ferocious howl of pain and rage. He charged toward Damon, his arm plowing forward, his hand an open claw to tear out his heart.

Fast as lightning, Damon leapt high in the air, flipping out of the way in time to hear the cry of pain that came from Kyros. He turned to see the two brothers, whose only loyalty had ever been to the other, staring into each other's eyes in stunned horror. Theron's fur-covered arm had been launched into Kyros' chest nearly elbow deep, his hand clutching the torn, but still beating heart. Though a Lycan couldn't be killed unless his heart was crushed and his head ripped completely off, Kyros was no doubt wishing he *could* die to stop the pain.

"I will kill him for you, brother." He heard Theron whisper before ripping his arm out of a squealing Kyros and launching himself at Damon with impossible speed. His eyes were red with bloodlust, his fangs dripping in his gaping jaw.

Damon felt the blood flooding down his leg, his body still weakened by whatever poison they had injected him with. He wasn't able to sidestep swiftly enough to avoid the move from Theron as he landed, pinning him to the ground with his angry weight.

He bucked off the larger Lycan but he knew his only hope of winning at this point was to fully change. Though he still hesitated, it was the only way. In that form, just as in his human one, he would be bigger and stronger than the crazed Theron. Before he had a chance, however, Theron's revenge was interrupted.

"Well, this is a surprise. Damon Arkadios, you are just too stubborn for your own good." Theron was tossed by some invisible force and thrown back to land beside his mewling brother.

Damon rolled up as quickly as he could, turning his head to catch the gaze of the smiling stranger.

A tall, well-muscled man who looked to be in his early thirties, with long, golden-brown hair that swung freely to his waist and a jagged silver scar across his left cheek. His arms were casually crossed as he shook his head chidingly. By his scent alone, Damon could tell he was Archon. But who?

"You could have ended this fight an hour ago if you'd fully shifted."

Damon raised his brow at the lecturing tone. "And you are...?"

The man threw back his head, his hair flying as he laughed aloud. He held his hands out at his sides, drawing Damon's attention to the strange, almost iridescent material of his dark outfit; the mandarin collar and loophole buttons on top reminding Damon of Raj's usual style of dress.

"Don't you recognize me?" He looked over at the two huddled masses in the corner, his eyes glinting with sudden menace. "Don't any of you recognize me?"

Seeing the confusion on Damon's face, he relented. "I've been watching you for so long that I forgot I was only a babe when last we met." Eyes, shining golden like his father's, twinkled. "I am Nyctimus, son of Zeus."

Damon stood, stunned, as he heard his brothers whimpering in renewed terror. Their bruised and battered bodies were human once more, attempting to crawl from the room. Nyctimus ignored them, focusing on Damon.

"Being half Archon is an amazing thing. They're fairly advanced. All that's left of my...*cutting* experience is this." He pointed to the single scar on his otherwise whole and perfect frame.

"You saved me, Damon. When you warned my father what Lycaon had planned." Theron's head looked up sharply as the man continued.

"And for your boon, what did he do? Went off half-cocked, putting the entire town under his bloody ridiculous curse, you included." Nyctimus sounded disgusted with his father's actions.

"Since it couldn't be undone, I watched and waited for a chance to repay you. And today is the day." His golden eyes gleamed as he rubbed his hands together in anticipation. "Now let's finish these two and take you to your woman."

Damon jerked his head up at these words. "You know where Meru is?" The other man nodded.

Damon looked over at Theron and Kyros. Saw through eyes that had seen countless ages come and go. Saw them for the pitiful creatures they had, after all, always been.

"Leave them. Take me to my mate."

Nyctimus looked at the man he had secretly considered his brother, in wonder. Born a slave, tortured without end and then given immortality under a demonic curse, Damon had cause to be bitter and vengeful.

Through it all, however, Nyctimus had only seen honor, Damon's constant struggle to hold dominion over his Lycan half, to use it to help rather than harm. He knew of no Archon who would turn the other cheek at such treatment. He shrugged, a little thrown as he walked over to Damon with the intent to flash away.

Theron, practically forgotten as he held the body of a mangled, moaning Kyros in his arms, let out a shout. "I *will* kill you, Damon! I won't rest until your heart is crushed in my hands. There won't always be someone around to save you.

And before you die, you'll watch your precious Meru suffer the same fate as your tattooed whore of a mother!"

Damon felt rage like a tidal wave rush through his body, but before he could take a step, Nyctimus let loose two brilliant bolts of light from his fingertips. Theron and Kyros were there one moment, two piles of ash on the ground in the next.

Apparently there was one other way to kill a Lycan. The Archon way.

"I'm actually glad he said that. I feel better now, don't you?" Damon was frozen with surprise. He looked sideways at the long-haired demigod.

"You're kind of a scary guy, aren't you, Nyctimus?" Damon asked, only half joking.

"Absolutely." He said right before they disappeared. "And call me Nyc."

He'd flashed them to an open field. When Damon looked at him in question, Nyctimus sighed. "The *Sauros* took Meru to Nimue."

"Nimue? But isn't she trapped in—"

"*Vorago*." Nyc nodded. "The area of chaos between our dimensions. The Council put her there, knowing she would never be able to escape it. Of course, they never imagined that she would find a way to work her mischief from the inside."

Damon felt true fear for the first time. Meru wasn't even on Earth. At least, not the same plane. And that crazy, power hungry Nimue had her in her clutches. The *Sauros* were following *her* orders? "How is that possible?"

"Trust me, from what I've heard, it's more than possible. The council's meeting about it as we speak. And while they are taking their sweet time trying to decide whether or not the fact that Meru is human should affect their decision to stop that lunatic, Meru could die."

Damon looked into Nyc's shining eyes for a moment. "What do I do?"

"Well, here's the tough part. The void is a surreal, infinitely confusing place. Even for Archon's. That's what makes it such a perfect prison. If you had fully mated with the woman, this wouldn't be an issue. As soon as I opened a doorway to *Vorago*, you'd be able to sense her, talk to her, track her. As it is now, only in full Lycan form will your senses be strong enough to catch her scent. Maybe." He looked as if he was expecting an argument. Damon didn't flinch.

"There is *also* the fact that a full shift will help to rid your system of that liquid silver concoction they pumped through your veins—as well as the nasty nick on your leg."

More silence. Nyc put his hands on his hips in aggravation.

"You aren't going to argue?" In answer, Damon let the ripple of the change overcome him. He felt the long forgotten cracks of elongating bone and stretching muscle, the tingling growth of the thick black pelt and the full extension of claws and teeth. It didn't hurt nearly as much as he remembered.

The wolf sat beside him in his mind, howling with the joy of acceptance, the completeness of the joining.

Damon still had total control, the power he now felt coursing through him his to command. Never had his senses been so acute, his instincts so honed. He let out a strange garbled laugh through the furred muzzle. He was laughing at himself for his pointless fears, laughing from the sheer pleasure of being whole.

He stood before Nyctimus, a fully shifted Lycan.

"This must be some woman." Nyc muttered as he began moving his hand in the air, making the strange symbols that would open Damon's way. "No change for three thousand plus years, not even a minute ago when your own brother was about to rip you open. Say the name Meru and, poof...wolf central."

A glowing circle the size of a door appeared in the field before them. Damon made a move to stalk toward it but Nyc intercepted him. "If I could come with you, I would. Technically, only members of The Council are allowed to enter unchallenged. Not even your team, the *Fianna*, can go into this place safely. Their Magick would be sensed immediately, as will yours. The repercussions for breaking that rule could be death. I have a feeling you, my brave brother, are willing to chance it." This last was said with admiration.

"Nimue has never been a match for another Archon but she *is* still an Archon. Be careful."

Damon's wolf like form nodded in understanding before launching himself into the light. He broke into a run as soon as he hit solid ground, the voice inside his head chanting, *Meru. Meru. Meru.*

* * * * *

"You really have no sense of humor at all."

Meru looked toward the voice, her screams dying as the illusion that had been surrounding her disappeared. For a moment she had really thought she was being devoured by flame. This was one sick woman, she thought bitterly, the tear tracks slowly drying on her cheeks.

She had never been more grateful for Aunt Lily's gift. She could feel the torc's soothing energy throughout Nimue's torture. She recalled what her aunt had said, that it couldn't protect her from everything, but it could help. Meru couldn't imagine how much worse this experience would be without it.

"Why are you doing this?"

"Because I can?" She laughed. "Because I'm bored? Because there's nothing else to do in this dull void? Because I am a goddess *and they can't treat me like this forever?*" She shouted the last at the ceiling, as if she were trying to be heard by some unseen force.

"I mean, why am I *here*? What do you want from me? Why send the *Sauros* after my family?"

"Oh that." She waved her hand flippantly. "I'm supposed to kill you. Painfully. He said it's the only way to stop the prophecy. Well, not the painfully part. That was just a bonus."

"Who?" Meru jumped on her last words, trying to ignore the killing her painfully part. "Who said it was the only way?"

"Never mind. Anyway, I thought about it. But I really think my idea is better." She walked toward the still bound Meru, obviously wanting to share her brilliance with an appreciative audience.

"I think Áine would just find another way to let everyone know about the prophecy if I killed you now, don't you? She always found a way. Perfect little Druid bitch." She muttered to herself for a moment.

"So I thought, why not keep you alive? You can call the book to you, read it and tell me everything I need to know to ensure that none of it comes to pass. Then they'll all see how foolish they were to underestimate me."

Wow, Meru thought. She was completely delusional. But she wasn't about to tell her it was a crazy idea, not when it bought her a bit more time to figure her way out of this madhouse.

"So, how did *He* find out about the prophecy, anyway?" She remembered what Myrddin had told her about the spell, and she was curious, despite her fear.

"He knew nothing." She crossed her arms smugly. "I was there when Áine was creating that blasted thing. And wasn't Myrddin just swooning all over himself, drooling over how amazing and self-sacrificing she was."

She sounded jealous. "What about the spell Myrddin—"

"The fool! He told me all about it. Didn't think I was smart enough to understand. Thought I could learn something. But I *did* understand. And I was ready." Her murky eyes took on an odd sheen.

"I wrapped a counter spell around myself. So I wouldn't forget." She shrugged uncomfortably as she continued. "It didn't work exactly as I planned. I forgot along with everyone else for a while, until a little over a year ago."

Nimue looked happy again, playing with her skirts like a pleased little girl as she continued. "When *He* found me again, I was able to tell him all I knew. Bits and pieces instead of the entire prophecy but it was enough. He was so happy with me that he told me about his plan for our future together. He even sent me servants as a gift for my brilliance."

Sent her servants? This mysterious *"He"* was the one who'd given her the *Sauros*? Meru had a sinking feeling that she now knew who *he* was. Enlil. Just then, her eyes caught a shadow of swift movement near the door.

"Oh, company! Thorny...greet our guest." Meru's heart tripped as she watched Allen turn at Nimue's command, the slits of his yellow eyes widening at what he saw. A Lycan, his chest heaving as if he'd been running for miles, was standing in the doorway.

He was a dark as night giant with ink black fur and some of the sharpest fangs she'd ever seen. Meru tried to get a better look from her position against the wall, only to find he was staring straight back at her. With Damon's eyes!

"Wh — what exactly do you want me to do, Mistress?" The *Sauros* took a cautious step back, his movements slow, eyes never wavering from the muscular beast that faced him.

"What do you mean? He told me you were smarter now, new and improved. You've failed me too many times, slave. Kill him now and all is forgiven. Disobey and I will tell your Lord."

Damon ignored their conversation, his dark, swirling eyes never straying from where Meru hovered, strapped to the wall.

She felt his gaze like a physical caress, relief and fear fighting for control inside her. He froze when he saw the large bruise on her cheek, the growl building from his chest, his eyes turning toward a quaking Thorne with a ferocious roar.

All his cocky arrogance gone without any backup to protect him, Allen turned to run, his hand reaching for the Archon transport in his pocket.

"How dare you?" Nimue's shout of outrage at his defection was lost in his horror-choked scream as the fully transformed Damon caught him easily in his grip.

Meru couldn't blink as the two began to struggle. Allen was no match for the Lycan, regardless of his threatening-looking talons. Damon tossed him across the room, turning to head for Meru, obviously intent on releasing her. Allen, seizing his opportunity, ran toward him, something silver glinting in his clawed hand.

"Damon!"

Before she could blink, it was over. She watched as the *Sauros* fell silent to the floor, his throat ripped open, an expression of surprise frozen on his face at his ignoble end. Damon looked at her over his shoulder, regret in his eyes at what she'd witnessed.

"Well, don't just stand there, silly. It's rude. Especially after making such a mess." Meru gasped as Damon seemed to fly through the air, hovering a few feet away from her, being controlled by a sneering Nimue.

He tried to fight her pull, his fur-covered muscles rippling with the effort. He seemed to push through the air that held him aloft, swiping his extended claw so close to Nimue's face that her hair rustled. The Archon just rolled her eyes.

"I guess if you want to do something right..." She made a motion with her hand and Damon began to howl in excruciating pain, wounds erupting on his beastlike form as if he was being beaten by some unseen attacker.

"No!" Meru screamed, struggling against the cuffs that held her securely to the wall. "*Please*, Nimue!"

"Don't call me that! *Myrddin's* the only one who ever called me that! Wanting me to love and care for you pathetic humans like he did. Loving you more than he ever loved me!"

the insane beauty stomped her feet and threw back her braided hair angrily. "My name is Ninmah!"

Ninmah? Meru thought wildly. But Ninmah was Enlil and Enki's— *Oh no.* "Ninmah, please don't do this! If you hurt him, I won't follow your brilliant plan! They'll never know how smart you are!"

Ninmah—Nimue paused in her torture, the noises coming from Damon subsiding into quiet groans. She looked over at Meru thoughtfully for a moment before giggling. "I just had the greatest idea for a game."

Horror closed her throat. Her last game had been to make Meru believe she was burning to death!

The cuffs at her wrists and ankles came loose and Meru was floating through the air toward a gold-leafed table beside the largest of the gilded mirrors. And that's when she saw it. The Cup.

"Obviously *I* can't do anything with it...but I thought it would be fun if you did." Ninmah waggled her fingers, and the Cup rose to where Meru was floating above it. She grabbed it, closing her hands around the thick stem.

"It's a ridiculous thing, isn't it? It doesn't give you any powers, it can't make you disappear and it certainly won't stop me from killing you. Leave it to that peace loving Danu to make something so worthless." She rolled her eyes.

"Okay, here's the game. You ask that ridiculous little mud cup how I'm going to kill you after I take care of your boyfriend here. Then you can tell me. I have to admit I'm certainly curious. There are so many choices."

Meru looked down into the empty goblet. Ninmah was seriously unhinged.

Hadn't she just told her that she'd planned to keep her alive to translate the Book? But for once, her lunacy worked in Meru's favor. She knew exactly what she needed to ask. She didn't care if Ninmah killed her when it was over. She just had to find a way to save Damon. There had to be a way.

The Cup filled with crystal clear water right before her eyes. She took a breath, asked her question silently and drank. Time seemed to stop as her mind expanded. Everything was suddenly so clear. She knew exactly what she had to do, as if she'd done it all before.

The Cup of Inspiration, its mission finally fulfilled, shattered into a showering cascade of light…disappearing once more into the mists of time.

Meru smiled, her back to the mad Archon as she projected her voice across the room.

"In the name of Kronos, first leader of Archon, I call on the Archon Council to render judgment! Here in *Virago*, The Void, where interaction is *not* forbidden. I, Meru Tanner, Druid Priestess from the line of Áine, demand satisfaction. For her crimes against both dimensions, judge Ninmah!" The formal plea fell easily from her lips, the response instantaneous.

As she fell to the floor, Meru heard a shout of fear before the entire scene changed. All of the overdone furniture and freak show mirrors were gone, replaced by…nothing. It actually looked like the void she had called it.

She spotted Damon lying curled up on the ground, unconscious, and ran to his side. When she made sure he was still breathing, she looked up.

Nine Archons, four stunning men and five impossibly beautiful women, stood in a semicircle around Ninmah, who knelt piteously before them. Meru felt tears of relief fill her eyes as she saw a scowling Myrddin among their number.

"We have answered the Druid's call for justice." This from a beautiful black woman who, if the winged symbol around her neck was anything to go by, was none other than the Egyptian goddess, Isis.

"Ninmah, you were sent here for mischief against the Earth Dimension and *now* you've been found attempting to compound your crimes by your treacherous actions against your own kind. You ignored the laws of the Archons and interfered with another's Magick for nefarious purpose. Are you ready to be judged?"

Ninmah shook her head wildly in denial, her braids whipping against her flesh painfully.

Myrddin stepped forward and addressed the other council members. "I ask The Council to consider allowing me the right of questioning. As the Archon whose Magick she interfered with...and as her husband's brother."

Meru squeaked, covering her mouth quickly with her hands as Myrddin sent her a quelling look. She was just getting used to calling him Myrddin. Was the professor actually saying that he was Enlil's brother Enki?

Her eyes closed as she leaned her head against Damon's silky pelt. She gave up. This was too confusing.

Isis raised a brow. "Do you think she would actually talk to you? The man she believes so wronged her affections? The man who confined her husband to his inescapable prison?"

"It's not inescapable!" Ninmah screeched. "Not for him! He's talked to me. To others! He has a plan! He—"

Meru looked up just as Ninmah made the most terrifying sound she had ever heard in her life.

The Archons around her went rigid in shock as they watched.

It seemed a storm of icy wind had enveloped Ninmah's body, and in seconds she was frozen. She looked like a perfect sculpture, kneeling there. Even her braids had been frozen where they'd flown, sticking up in icy spikes around her head. Then, just as quickly as she'd frozen...she broke. Shards of ice littered the floor in front of the council. Ninmah was no more.

"Lord of the Air." A male Archon muttered, looking around nervously, obviously disconcerted by what he'd witnessed.

Isis turned to Myrddin. "It would seem, old friend, that your brother has found a crack in that impenetrable prison you created for him."

Myrddin was about to respond when Isis caught Meru's wide gaze and raised her hand to silence him. "Druid Priestess, your work here is done. Take your Lycan and go in peace."

Myrddin looked into Meru's eyes, sending a message she couldn't decipher in her shock and smiled. "I just knew you would do well," he whispered, repeating the phrase he'd said in the library. It seemed to her like a long ago memory. So much had happened in the past few days.

"Take him home, dear girl, take him home." And with a wave of his hand, Meru and Damon flashed out of sight.

Chapter Twelve

She wobbled, disoriented for a moment and a little nauseous. That's it, she thought grumpily, coming to a firm decision. No more of this flashing business. Why these people couldn't just use their feet or take a cab, she'd never know.

Her musings were interrupted by a groaning Damon. Her eyes flew to where he lay, unconscious, on a bed beside her. Bed?

She looked around the room. Where were they? This certainly wasn't Myrddin's house. Another groan and a slight grimace of pain had Meru losing interest in her location. All that mattered was tending the man before her.

No longer in his Lycan form, Damon looked like he'd been in a war. His nude body was battered, dried blood covering his leg from what looked to be a set of swiftly healing claw marks.

Her heart ached at the thought of him suffering. She looked around until she spotted the bathroom, scrounging for the needed supplies.

She cleaned up the blood and tended his wounds with quick efficiency, trying to ignore the bare, muscled flesh beneath her hands.

When she realized she was dreamily caressing his already clean chest with the washcloth, she forced herself to step back. She tucked him under the light cotton sheet before heading out of the room so he could rest.

Feeling dirty and utterly exhausted, she decided to jump in the shower before exploring. She let her mind go blank as the hot water pelted her skin. She didn't pay attention to the tears of release mixed with the droplets of water on her face, the chilled trembling in her limbs brought on by the shocking events this day had wrought. By the time she emerged, an hour had passed and she had started to feel human again.

She found a large, masculine robe hanging against the bathroom door, sliding into it before she peeked in on Damon, who still appeared to be sound asleep. She stared for long moments, contenting herself with watching his chest rise and fall slowly.

He was alive.

She walked up beside him, brushing a strand of silky, dark hair off his forehead lovingly before heading downstairs for a little light snooping. She was astounded by what she found.

This was a house straight out of her fondest daydreams, with high-beamed ceilings and a bright, airy feel.

The décor, distinctly masculine, was all dark woods and leather furniture, with simple lines and not a lot of clutter. There were rough-hewn bookshelves against the far wall, full to bursting with paperback novels, hardcovers and magazines.

The focal point of the room was the massive fireplace, with a stained driftwood mantle, a gigantic flat screen television moonlighting as the only artwork above it. She even spied an X-box on the floor, shoved against the wall. Yep, definitely a man's retreat. But a beautiful one.

She walked through the large, open kitchen. The industrial-size stainless steel appliances and latest in cooking gadgetry led her to believe that whoever lived here truly enjoyed cooking. But it was the floor-to-ceiling windows taking up the entire front of the house that she loved the most. She was drawn to them. The scene they revealed to her was shocking.

Stepping through the glass door, she walked toward the edge of the wide, wooden deck. Beyond her was the landscape of her visions, where she had met and spoken with Danu.

She saw the stream in the distance, the emerald field and fairy mound, looked up at the too exquisite to be real blue of the sky. She was actually here at the house she had wondered about in her dreams!

Looking around, almost expecting to see the ethereal blonde woman striding toward her, she pinched her arm beneath the thick terry of the robe. She was awake, which could only mean that Myrddin had flashed them to—

"Welcome to Ireland, Meru. Welcome to my home."

She turned at the sound of his husky voice, her heart in her throat as she gazed at Damon. All the love she felt for him, all that they'd been through over the past few days, the fact that he had almost *died*...all merged into a single driving need in her mind. She had to touch him.

Black eyes blazed as he opened his arms at her unspoken plea, lifting her up as she flung herself against him. Her hands sifted eagerly through his hair, legs wrapped tight around his waist as if afraid he might let her go.

Damon groaned at the feel of her finally back in his arms where she belonged. He took her mouth in a kiss filled with all the urgent passion and adoration inside him.

When he'd woken to find himself alone in his own bed, for one groggily insane moment he'd imagined it had all been a dream. The prophecy, the Cup, Meru's abduction. Everything.

His soul had nearly wept at the idea that he hadn't found his mate after all, hadn't gotten a chance to know her, to taste her lips, the sweet honey of her sex. To thank her for the wholeness she had brought into his life.

Less than a heartbeat later, he'd woken enough to become aware of her evocative and achingly familiar scent as it wrapped around his Lycan soul. She was *here*!

He took the stairs in a single, joy-filled leap, heedless of his unclothed state. He'd found her looking in awe at the scenery around her. He'd owned this land forever. Its isolation, not to mention the helpful spell of hiding Finn had cloaked it with, had made it the perfect home base for the men. No tourist could see it, no *Dark* could penetrate it and it was within sight of the doorway to the Tuatha's Realm…and the North Portal.

Seeing Meru standing there, her dark curls shifting in the light summer breeze, the scent of lavender from the field beyond reminiscent of her own natural fragrance, Damon thought he might have actually built this home for her. For his mate. As if some part of him knew he would find her.

He'd looked at her, standing there in nothing but his robe, and knew he had to make her his in truth. Nyc's words, as well as the advice of Raj and Hawk, burned worriedly into his brain. After all that had happened with Nimue and the *Sauros*, he knew that the only way to ensure her continued safety was to mark her and join her life to his.

She'd come into his embrace and his body had tightened with desire, the wolf inside baying in lustful agreement with his plan. Both sides of his nature focusing as one on the small, curvaceous armful he now held.

He felt her wet, naked pussy pressed against his bare flesh through the opening of the robe, robbing him of breath and hardening his already stiff cock to a near painful level of need. Gods, he *needed* her now.

He turned to bring her inside, possessively determined to see her surrounded by his things, on his bed. Meru's face nuzzled his neck as he entered the living room, licking the salted cord of his neck, sucking the lobe of his ear in her hot little mouth.

The soft fur rug in front of the fireplace caught Damon's eye. His bed or his rug? As she squirmed against him, the loose robe opening at her movements, pressing the soft, full globes of her breast against his chest, rubbing the tight points of her nipples over his burning skin, he decided they'd traveled far enough.

He had been planning on romancing her, telling her how he felt. He wanted to explain the mating ritual to her in caring detail, answer all her questions. The heat that always flared up between them, however, roared to life with a vengeance as he laid her down, quickly stripping her of his robe and kneeling between her creamy thighs. The scent of her need hit him with the force of a hurricane, her excited whimpers as he licked one taut, juicy nipple nearly driving him mad with desire.

She arched sharply at the feel of his mouth opening wide around her breast, as if he were trying to suck her down and swallow her whole. He nibbled, he laved, sucking her pebbled peak hard against the roof of his mouth. Ravenous sounds emerged from his throat as his mouth traveled across her chest to the breast he'd been neglecting, offering equal treatment.

Crying out, she gripped his shoulders, her fingernails cutting into his flesh. She felt each pull of his mouth send fiery bursts of need to her core, her molten juices soaking the lips of her sex at the sensation. She ran her hands over every part of him she could reach, bending her knees and wrapping her legs around his waist, desperate to feel him fully against her.

"More," she sobbed. "Please, Damon. I need you. I need you *now*."

He growled low against her breast, pressing his hips against hers. His cock pulsed against her swollen clit as he took her hands in his, pressing them flat against the floor. Damon raised his head and looked into her eyes, his own a brilliant black, burning with ferocious intent.

The hard edge of desire on his face softened slightly, replaced by a look of such indescribable wonder that her heart fluttered at the sight. He swallowed, his long lashes shielding his expression for a moment.

"Love you, Meru." His voice lowered as he lifted his eyes to hers. "I love you. *Mate*."

She gasped, and then whispered softly, "I love you too, Damon. *My* mate."

It was as if sunlight had broken through the darkness. That was the only way she could describe the expression that erupted on his face at her words. She knew his joy was a match for hers. That he was her match in every way.

His gaze heated once more as he felt the tiny, inadvertent thrusts of her hips against his, her body still tingling with need. He smiled a devil's grin, made all the more dangerous and sexy by his sharp, lengthening canines.

The tip of his weeping cock nudged her pussy, causing her to moan and arch more fully against him. The feel of his skin against hers was indescribable. Heavenly.

Damon slid through her dewy sex, coating his shaft with her juices, the erotic sensation causing her to thrash and writhe against him.

He teased them both without mercy, thrusting slowly between her trembling thighs, lightly pressing against her before sliding away, causing her pussy to spasm in aching need; longing for him to fill her. She jerked against his hold on her hands. She wanted to touch him, needed to touch him.

She looked into his blackened eyes, her own moist with desire, and he groaned, as if the feelings had suddenly become too much for him as well. He released her struggling hands, only to raise his body away from hers, flipping her over to land on her hands and knees before him.

She leaned down on her elbows, parting her thighs wide and wiggling her hips slightly in invitation. The swollen folds of her sopping sex lay open to his heated gaze, begging him to take what was his.

"Are you trying to tempt me to lose control? Are you being a 'bad girl' again?"

The memory of the first time he'd called her that and the delicious punishment he'd inflicted made her shiver. His broad palms cupped the silken globes, stilling her movements in a warning that felt more like a caress, and she smiled.

"I can take whatever you dish out," she gasped bravely, her body instinctively pushing into his hands.

He chuckled as she felt his thick fingers slipping through her arousal, soaking the digits as he growled hungrily. "So sweet, baby. I want to cover myself in your honey. Drink it down and swim in your sweet juices." She sobbed out a moan, her hips arching instinctively higher at his carnal words.

Damon covered her body with his own, his cock jerking against her as his words grated harsh with need in her ear. "I need to fuck you, Meru. To *love* you. To make you mine in everyway. I can't lose you again. Will you let me, baby?"

Anything. Meru nodded, trying to entice him to take her, but he just held her tighter. "Do you know what that means to a Lycan, Meru? Do you know what I'll want to do? What I'll *have* to do?"

In answer, she raised one arm from the floor, pulled her hair back over one shoulder with a shaking hand and tilted her neck invitingly.

The torc glimmered in the soft light and Damon's large frame trembled against her as he stared in awe at the trust her action implied. The trust she had given him from the first. His heart burst with love for this amazing woman. *His* woman. His Meru.

His jaw clenched with restraint as he entered her, her drenched pussy clenching around him like a tight, gripping fist. He pressed his lips against her neck, growling uncontrollably against her as he thrust deep into her silken heat, unable to go slow.

She cried out as she felt her tissues stretch around him, trying to accommodate his massive length. She felt his tongue lapping at her pale skin, laving sensuously as he filled her with each powerful thrust of his cock.

She felt him expanding inside of her, the body around her growing larger as the wolf came to the fore. The animal sounds of rapture coming from Damon caused Meru to moan with desire, soaking them both with her arousal as she greedily tilted her hips, pulling him deeper with every downward glide.

My Lycan, she thought with a joyous whimper as she buried her face into the soft fur of the rug beneath her. With each pounding drive of his hips, she felt the veins and ridges of his engorged shaft as he filled her to bursting, molding and reshaping her with his need.

Harder and faster, the room filled with the sounds of their heated coupling and pleasured groans. She rose up on her elbows to push back against him, crying out his name as she joined him stroke for stroke.

His clawed hands left her hips, lowering to cover hers on the floor in a show of gentle domination. He growled softly once more against her neck as his hips slammed relentlessly against her own. It was primal, earthy and elemental. She loved it. She loved him. He groaned her name in a garbled, guttural voice, his fangs grazing the curve of her shoulder.

She came in a strong volcanic blast just as she felt the quick, painfully erotic lunge of his teeth piercing her neck. He roared against her, his open mouth sucking hard as he swelled impossibly inside her, causing her to erupt once more as he pumped stream, after endless stream of cum into her quivering flesh.

He gripped her tightly to him, holding her up when she would have collapsed on the floor. He tongued her neck, healing the wound and savoring her taste.

She could feel him, still hard despite his recent climax, still pumping slowly inside her. Dazed, she looked at him over her shoulder and raised one eyebrow in question. Damon merely smiled and lifted himself off her back.

He pressed one gentle, but firm, hand between her shoulder blades, and her body began to tingle with renewed arousal as she allowed him to position her body into a pose of helpless supplication, her hips high in the air, thighs spread, torso pressed flat against the rug.

Continuing to thrust slow and steady inside her, his fingers slid around her hip to gently press her pulsing clit, slipping in their mingled juices until his fingers were coated with it.

Meru, whose eyes had been closed, her mind focused on his tender caresses, jerked in surprise as one blunt, wet finger pressed firmly between her cheeks, circling the pink rosette teasingly before slowly sliding into her ass.

She must have made a noise. "I told you, baby. I told you I wanted to fuck you here. So tight. Such a sweet, tight ass. It's gonna feel so good, Meru, I promise."

She was in no shape to argue. To be honest, she'd never been so turned on in her entire life. Just the thought of sharing something so intimate, so forbidden, with this man had her pushing her hips backward, the unused muscles stretching to accommodate him as he added a second finger to the first.

She could feel him everywhere. His cock as it thrust deep into her womb, his thick fingers pushing deeper, stretching her anus. It was shocking, the feeling of fullness. She moaned and laid her forehead weakly against the soft fur of the rug, trying to breathe through the sensations. It felt indescribably wicked. "Damon, oh, it feels *so* good."

Her back arched at the indescribable fullness. Pain, yes, as the thick head of his cock breached the tight ring of muscles, but pleasure as well. A pleasure so intense it shot up her spine, an electric zap that caused her body to flush and tremble in reaction. She bit her lip and tasted blood.

"So tight. So tight around my cock. Ah gods, *Meru*."

He roared as her muscles flexed around the steel of his cock and she thought she could actually sense the moment he lost his vaunted control, his hips rocking against hers with a near-bruising force as he finally let go.

When she felt his teeth clamp onto her shoulder once more, claiming her in the most elemental, primal way, she cried out in ecstasy. She bucked backward against him, driving him deeper still as she shattered in a thousand pieces. It was devastating. It was wonderful.

She saw black spots dance before her eyes moments before she heard him calling her name as he emptied himself once more inside her, collapsing next to her as if he too had been devastated by the experience.

She allowed herself to spread into an exhausted heap on the floor, wondering when the shaking would stop, when she felt herself being unceremoniously flipped over.

"Meru. Are you all right?"

She felt his hand on her face and realized her cheeks were soaked with tears. She smiled weakly and nodded. He looked carefully into her eyes, the worried look in his own fading and a smile tugging at his lips at whatever he found there. He studied the wound on her neck, already closing from the healing ministrations of his tongue, and let out an inward whoop of joyous relief.

All the fears about control were banished now. He had been overwhelmed with sensation, the wolf reveling in her blood, drinking it down greedily. But even the instincts of the wolf, ever protective of his mate, would only allow him to take so much. He had joined them together in the most unbreakable bond of his kind. They were mated. Their souls and minds merged.

Mate, he thought possessively.

"You better not forget it, either." The voice rose up from a cloud of curls as she slumped, boneless in his arms. His eyebrows rose and he cuddled her closer, seeing her sated smile and chuckling softly.

Can you hear me, Meru?

"Of course I can hear you. You've stolen my muscle coordination, not my hearing."

Open your eyes, baby.

She slowly did as he requested, blinking in surprise when he repeated his question. "Umm…your lips didn't move."

You are my mate. We can communicate mentally now.

"Finn talked to me telepathically."

His eyes narrowed. *Don't think about other men at a time like this.*

She giggled, pulling him down for a long leisurely kiss. *You're so sensitive. Why on earth would I think about that Faerie when I have such a big, strong, lusty wolf as my mate?*

I love you, baby.

She knew.

* * * * *

Three weeks later…

Meru sat on the deck of her new home, her smiling gaze fixed on the picturesque view that surrounded her. Ireland felt like coming home. She didn't miss Houston at all. Everything and everyone she loved was right here. Including her family.

The silver eyed Archon had arrived within hours of their mating, interrupting a very sexy, very *naked* cooking lesson. After she'd dressed and the color in her cheeks had faded, Myrddin had told them that everyone was fine and that they would arrive after giving them a few days alone to recover. She rolled her eyes, imagining the scene clearly, impressed that Myrddin had been able to get her aunt and Sheridan to agree to the wait.

He didn't hesitate to answer all of her questions about what she'd witnessed. She'd been fascinated by the story.

When he'd first arrived through the portal, he'd been known as Enki. Enlil was his brother and Ninmah his brother's young, troubled bride, for whom Enki had always harbored a protective, brotherly affection.

Enlil had abused his power in unspeakable ways, determined to destroy any member of the human race who would not bow to him. Messing with the natural evolution of mankind and even utilizing the darker forces of Magick in an attempt to rule over the other Archons. Once that line had been crossed, Enki had been chosen to imprison him.

Guilty over his brother's actions and his own arrogance in believing it was right to play with the fate of another race, Enki had gone to Danu and her people for guidance and enlightenment.

They helped him a great deal, offering him solace and privacy, but he couldn't completely accept their road of isolation, either. He couldn't stop thinking about the vulnerable mortals that dwelt in this dimension.

In order to help them, he had become Myrddin. Eschewing his name and the power it evoked, he chose instead to educate, aid and even live among the race that his family had tried to destroy.

He'd tried to teach the lost Ninmah as well, but she had been poisoned by Enlil's hatred and he'd had been too blind to see it. In the end, she had grown so jealous of Myrddin's attention to the "inferior race", she'd snapped. She had hurt a lot of people before she too was incarcerated.

Damon had been just as amazed by the tale as she. He guiltily told Meru that he had been caught up in his own struggles for so many years, it hadn't even occurred to him that Myrddin had suffered as well.

After he'd satisfied Meru's curiosity, Damon asked Myrddin about Nyctimus. The older man looked sheepish. "I'm sorry I didn't tell you about him. I knew Zeus used his abilities to heal the child, he *was* half Archon after all, but I wasn't sure how you'd react to the knowledge at first. After a few thousand years, you still didn't look ready to discuss the past, so I held my tongue." Myrddin chuckled.

"I should've known Nyc would come to you. He didn't speak to his father for centuries after finding out all the facts of that night. As far as he was concerned, Zeus should have found a way to save you and your mother…his as well, instead of reacting first and thinking later. Come to think of it," Myrddin lowered his voice with a smirk, "Nyc *still* barely tolerates that pompous old bolt thrower."

Realizing it was confession time, she flushed guiltily as she caught Myrddin's eye. "I failed. Áine's Cup shattered. I didn't ask how to stop what was coming. All I could think of was finding a way to stop Ninmah from killing Damon."

Damon's shocked eyes fell on her, a moment before he drew her tenderly backward into his arms. Myrddin took her hand. "Meru." She looked up slowly.

"Do you regret your decision?"

"No." Meru didn't hesitate.

"Neither would Áine. For all you know, you did exactly what she knew you would. You used the Cup for love instead of for greed or power. It sounds just like something she would do."

Shortly after their conversation, Myrddin left. He promised he would keep everyone away for as long as he could.

The entourage had come flashing in after four days of blissful, sex-filled solitude. A sort of mini-honeymoon before the in-laws descended, she'd jokingly told the scowling Damon.

Fletcher had arrived with Raj and Lily. Her aunt was over the moon about her "marriage" to Damon. Although she was already making noise about a full Druid wedding ceremony, just to make it official.

Lily thought Myrddin could perform the rites, though she insisted, looking at Meru with a conspirator's grin, she was going to have to go into town to purchase him a cowboy hat for the occasion. Meru laughed and Damon just looked confused as Fletcher informed her without expression that she'd be wiser to purchase one online, seeing as they were back in civilized Ireland and not the Wild West. Her eyes sparkled at the memory.

Beautiful, bookish Raj, that wonderful man, had brought her all the texts from Myrddin's library that she'd not had the time to look through. As a mating gift, he'd said with a gentle smile.

Sheridan, Finn and Val hadn't been far behind. Much to Kyle's regret, Sheridan had taken an extended leave of absence after all the negative press the family had received around the fire and the death of Lily's friend.

Thanks to Finn's "powers of persuasion", no charges had been filed against any of the women. The case was kept open, though Meru knew it would never be solved, and Sheridan was in no danger of losing her position. But she still felt she needed some time to sort through all the changes the last month had wrought in her life. Plus, she added, she'd never be able to stand being away from her mother or Meru for very long.

It was surprising to say the least. Sheridan loved her job. She loved being a cop. But when she'd arrived, her eyes suspiciously moist as she embraced Meru, threatening her with rug burns, swirlies and worse if she ever put herself in harm's way again, Meru decided not press her.

Though Finn and Val had been angry that they'd missed all the excitement, they were satisfied with hearing Meru and Damon tell their tale.

Over and over again.

She looked down at The Book of Veils, her hand caressing the soft texture in loving gratitude. She recalled the rune she'd drawn that last day at The Willow's Knot, the rune of New Beginnings. It had certainly been that. A whole new world had been opened up for her.

She felt a bit like she'd fallen down the rabbit hole, and indeed some of the losses were painful. But how could she regret a life full of adventure and Magick and love?

She wasn't sure if she'd have been able to overcome her challenges without the love and support of the women in her family. The strength and loyalty of Sheridan, the warmth and acceptance of Aunt Lily.

She traced the outline of her wolf's head torc, thinking of Áine and her mother Rose, whose love had come to aid her even from beyond the grave. And then, of course, there was Damon.

Damon had made her happier than she ever dreamed she could be. She knew that, together, they could handle anything that might come their way. She felt him kneel beside her chair, his hand resting over the soft curve of her belly.

Even another new beginning?

She should have guessed he'd know about that even before she did. He was Lycan, after all. She nodded and covered his hand with her own. A new life.

Opening the book, she looked at the partially finished prophecy before her. The last line of the verse related to her made her smile.

Her heart must find its mate 'neath a cursed moon
If she is to be saved.

Her mate. Her Lycan. He had saved her, his love had helped her to become stronger than she'd ever known she could be. Strong enough to save him in return. His hand squeezed her a bit tighter at her thoughts before he looked down at the book with startled eyes.

"Meru? Your book is writing something."

She looked down, not at all surprised to see fresh ink forming the words of the next section of the prophecy. Raj had been right. Her part in Áine's vision had to be fulfilled before the next could appear.

> *The eyes of the hawk watch over*
> *The daughter of my spirit.*
> *A guardian of human born,*
> *Pure and innocent in her power,*
> *Will seek and find the light no other can behold.*
> *The hawk of gold torn in two, made whole again*
> *When the key is found.*

"What's it say?"

She jumped as she and Damon both turned toward the voice. She rolled her eyes. He just kept popping up. Like an irritating Archon penny. Damon laughed and, traitor that he was, repeated her thought aloud to Nyctimus.

"Half Archon." He corrected with a grin, undeterred. "What's it say?" She couldn't help smiling. He and Damon had grown quite close over the past few weeks. Once they'd put the past behind them.

Nyctimus had sat Damon down and apologized formally for the unfair and thoughtless actions of his father. Damon told him that there was nothing to forgive. After all, he'd taken Meru's hand as he'd continued, if it had never happened, he would never have found his heart's true mate.

Since then, the two had been thick as thieves. They were the closest thing to brothers and she truly couldn't be happier at her growing, if unique, family unit.

"It says..." She stood, stretching as she walked Nyctimus and Damon toward the laughter coming from the house. The distinct sounds of that crazy video game they all loved were blasting from the living room. *Men.*

She would let them all have their fun for now. Soon enough she would have to share not only the newly revealed prophecy, but the information she'd received from Danu in her dream last night as well. It seemed their battle with Enlil and the *Dark* wasn't finished, not by a long shot.

"It says," She offered Nyc a smile, though Damon's gaze narrowed at the worried glimmer in her eyes. "That Val and Hawk are about to be two very busy Vikings."

Also by R.G. Alexander
ಸಿ

eBooks:
Lifting the Veil
Piercing the Veil
Who Needs Another Superhero?
Who Wants to Date a Superhero?

Print Books:
Who Loves a Supershero? *(anthology)*

About the Author

৩

Stolen away by a free spirited gypsy as a child, (though she still swears she's my mother) I spent my childhood roaming the countryside, meeting fascinating characters and having amazing adventures. As the perpetual "new kid", my friends more often than not were found between the pages of a book...and in my own imagination. I read everything I could get my hands on. At the age of 11, I read my first romance and I've been hooked ever since.

I've been a nurse, a lead vocalist in several bands, a published lyricist and even a returning student at University majoring in Anthropology and Mythology. Throughout all of my varied careers I would sigh as I read one fantasy-filled story after another saying, "Someday I want to write one of those." Until one day my husband said, "So do it." And I did. Now I can't imagine doing anything else.

R.G. Alexander welcomes comments from readers. You can find her website and email address on her author bio page at www.ellorascave.com.

Tell Us What You Think

We appreciate hearing reader opinions about our books. You can email us at Comments@EllorasCave.com.

Why an electronic book?

We live in the Information Age—an exciting time in the history of human civilization, in which technology rules supreme and continues to progress in leaps and bounds every minute of every day. For a multitude of reasons, more and more avid literary fans are opting to purchase e-books instead of paper books. The question from those not yet initiated into the world of electronic reading is simply: *Why?*

1. ***Price.*** An electronic title at Ellora's Cave Publishing and Cerridwen Press runs anywhere from 40% to 75% less than the cover price of the exact same title in paperback format. Why? Basic mathematics and cost. It is less expensive to publish an e-book (no paper and printing, no warehousing and shipping) than it is to publish a paperback, so the savings are passed along to the consumer.
2. ***Space.*** Running out of room in your house for your books? That is one worry you will never have with electronic books. For a low one-time cost, you can purchase a handheld device specifically designed for e-reading. Many e-readers have large, convenient screens for viewing. Better yet, hundreds of titles can be stored within your new library—on a single microchip. There are a variety of e-readers from different manufacturers. You can also read e-books on your PC or laptop computer. (Please note that Ellora's Cave does not endorse any specific brands.

You can check our websites at www.ellorascave.com or www.cerridwenpress.com for information we make available to new consumers.)

3. *Mobility.* Because your new e-library consists of only a microchip within a small, easily transportable e-reader, your entire cache of books can be taken with you wherever you go.

4. *Personal Viewing Preferences.* Are the words you are currently reading too small? Too large? Too... ANNOYING? Paperback books cannot be modified according to personal preferences, but e-books can.

5. *Instant Gratification.* Is it the middle of the night and all the bookstores near you are closed? Are you tired of waiting days, sometimes weeks, for bookstores to ship the novels you bought? Ellora's Cave Publishing sells instantaneous downloads twenty-four hours a day, seven days a week, every day of the year. Our webstore is never closed. Our e-book delivery system is 100% automated, meaning your order is filled as soon as you pay for it.

Those are a few of the top reasons why electronic books are replacing paperbacks for many avid readers.

As always, Ellora's Cave and Cerridwen Press welcome your questions and comments. We invite you to email us at Comments@ellorascave.com or write to us directly at Ellora's Cave Publishing Inc., 1056 Home Avenue, Akron, OH 44310-3502.

Make each day more EXCITING With our

Ellora's Cavemen Calendar

✢ www.EllorasCave.com ✢

Discover for yourself why readers can't get enough of the multiple award-winning publisher Ellora's Cave.

Whether you prefer e-books or paperbacks, be sure to visit EC on the web at www.ellorascave.com for an erotic reading experience that will leave you breathless.

CPSIA information can be obtained at www.ICGtesting.com
Printed in the USA
LVOW052033140612

286170LV00001B/202/P